SEVASTOPOL TALES

LEO TOLSTOY

TRANSLATED FROM THE RUSSIAN
BY NICOLAS PASTERNAK SLATER

PUSHKIN PRESS CLASSICS

Pushkin Press
Somerset House, Strand
London WC2R ILA

Sevastopol Tales was first published as *Sevastopolskiye rasskazy* in serial form in *Sovremennik*, 1855–56

First published by Pushkin Press in 2026

ISBN 13: 978-1-80533-260-2

A CIP catalogue record for this title is available from the British Library

The authorised representative in the EEA is eucomply OÜ, Pärnu mnt. 139b-14, 11317, Tallinn, Estonia, hello@eucompliancepartner.com, +33757690241

Cover image: *Trumpeter of the Hussars*, c. 1815–20 by Théodore Géricault

Designed and typeset by Tetragon, London
Printed and bound in the United Kingdom by Clays Ltd, Elcograf S.p.A.

Pushkin Press is committed to a sustainable future for our business, our readers and our planet. This book is made from paper from forests that support responsible forestry.

www.pushkinpress.com

1 3 5 7 9 8 6 4 2

PUSHKIN PRESS CLASSICS

SEVASTOPOL TALES

'What Tolstoy achieves—and what any fiction writer hopes to achieve—is, in fact, magic'

CLAIRE MESSUD

'All of Tolstoy's writing, fictional and non-fictional, is concerned with truth'

J.M. COETZEE

'If the world could write by itself, it would write like Tolstoy'

ISAAC BABEL

LEO TOLSTOY (1828–1910) was born into the Russian aristocracy, spent his youth in aimless dissolution, and joined the army in a bid to escape his gambling debts. *Sevastopol Tales*, based on his experience serving as an artillery officer in the Crimean War, helped to establish his fame as a writer in the 1850s. The war helped transform him into a passionate pacifist and social agitator, and his sense of moral purpose inspired his writing throughout his long life. He started a series of schools for the recently emancipated serfs of Russia, and published several literary masterpieces, including the novels *War and Peace* and *Anna Karenina*. Living in retirement on his ancestral estate, he gradually became a near-messianic figure, receiving literary, political and spiritual pilgrims, both lauded and persecuted by the Russian authorities. He was nominated five times for the Nobel Prizes in Literature and Peace, but never won.

NICOLAS PASTERNAK SLATER is the nephew of novelist Boris Pasternak. After retiring from his career as a doctor he turned to translation, and has published several highly praised versions of great Russian authors, including Pushkin, Dostoyevsky and Chekhov.

SEVASTOPOL TALES

Contents

Historical Note

In 1854–5, as a young officer, Tolstoy took part in the defence of Sevastopol during the siege of the city by mainly French and British forces. This was one of the turning points of the Crimean War. The *Sevastopol Tales* are fictionalized accounts inspired by his lived experience.

It may be useful to the reader to have an idea of the background to these *Tales*. Sevastopol lies on the southern shore of its harbour, an inlet of the Black Sea on the west coast of the Crimean peninsula. Across Sevastopol harbour is the North Side, relatively untroubled by the invaders; a pontoon bridge connects the North Side to the city on the south shore.

The harbour is sealed off from the Black Sea by two lines of Russian ships which have been scuttled to prevent enemy access. Tolstoy describes the masts of these sunken ships projecting above the surface of the bay. The guns were transferred to dry land and used in the defence of Sevastopol; they were fired by sailors, which explains the number of sailors fighting on land in Tolstoy's account.

The city is surrounded by a line of Russian fortifications, with a numbered series of strong points along them (the bastions). The fourth and fifth bastions lie to the south-west of the city; the Kornilov bastion (not numbered) is an important fortification on the south-east side, on an elevation called Malakhov Hill (or the Malakhov mound). All these bastions are facing French troops.

It is on Malakhov Hill that the last decisive action takes place. (After the French victory, a district of Paris was named Malakoff after this hill.)

SEVASTOPOL IN DECEMBER

DAWN IS ONLY just beginning to tinge the horizon above Mount Sapun; the deep-blue surface of the sea has already shed the darkness of night and awaits the first ray of sunlight to bring it out in a cheerful sparkle; a chilly mist blows in from the bay; the ground is bare of snow, all is black, but the biting frost of morning pinches your face and crackles underfoot; and only the distant, unceasing boom of the sea, interrupted now and then by echoing gunshots from Sevastopol, disturbs the morning quiet. The muffled sound of eight bells rings out on the nearby ships.

On the North Side, the daytime bustle slowly dispels the calm of night. Here a relief detachment of sentries marches by with a clatter of muskets; there a doctor is already hurrying to the hospital; further on, a soldier scrambles out of his dugout to splash his sunburnt face with icy water, turns towards the reddening east, hurriedly crosses himself and says a prayer; over there a tall, cumbersome camel-drawn *madzhara** creaks its way to the cemetery where its load of bloody corpses, piled almost to the top, will be buried... You walk on to the quay, where you are assailed by that peculiar smell of coal, manure, damp and beef; thousands of random objects—firewood, meat, gabions, flour, iron, and the like—lie in heaps by the quayside; soldiers from different regiments

* A cart with latticed sides.

mill around, with and without their kitbags and guns, smoking, swearing at one another, and manhandling heavy loads onto the steamer which is moored by the quayside with its steam up; small boats for hire, loaded with all sorts of passengers—soldiers, sailors, merchants, women—moor and cast off from the quayside.

'To the Grafskaya, your Honour? Come aboard.' Two or three retired sailors stand up in their boats to offer their services.

You pick the nearest boat, stepping over the half-decomposed carcass of a brown horse lying in the mud beside it, go aboard and make your way to the tiller. Now you have cast off. All around you, the sea is already gleaming in the morning sunlight; in front of you, an old sailor in a camel-hair overcoat and a tow-headed young lad are silently and doggedly working the oars. You look out at the enormous striped hulls of the ships scattered near and far over the bay, and the little black dots of boats moving across the sparkling azure water, and the beautiful bright buildings of the town across the bay, tinged pink in the rays of the morning sun; and the foamy white line of the boom, and the scuttled ships, with here and there a black masthead projecting forlornly out of the water, and far in the distance the enemy fleet, just visible on the crystal-clear skyline; and the frothing eddies and leaping salty bubbles raised by the oars; you listen to the regular beating of the oars, and hear the voices wafted to you across the water, and the majestic sounds of cannon fire in Sevastopol, which seems to you to be growing more intense.

The thought that you too are in Sevastopol cannot fail to fill your soul with a sense of manliness and pride, making your blood course faster through your veins…

'Your Honour! You're making straight for the *Constantine*!' says the old seaman, looking round to see the course you are steering. 'Bear a bit to starboard.'

'She's still got all her guns aboard,' remarks the tow-headed lad, casting an eye over the ship as you pass it.

''Course she has; she's new—Kornilov lived on board of her,' says the old man, also looking at the ship.

'My, just look at that one going off!' exclaims the boy after a long silence, gazing up at a spreading white cloud of smoke that has suddenly appeared high over the South Bay, accompanied by the sharp crack of an exploding mortar bomb.

'That's *him*, firing from his new battery today,' says the old man, spitting imperturbably into his hand. 'Well, press on, Mishka, let's get ahead of that longboat.' And our boat speeds ahead over the broad swell of the bay, and does indeed overhaul the heavy longboat loaded with sacks, awkwardly rowed by inexperienced soldiers; and we finally pull in alongside the Grafskaya quay, surrounded by a varied collection of other moored boats.

The quayside is crowded with a noisy, bustling throng of soldiers in grey, sailors in black and women in all sorts of colours. The women are selling bread rolls, Russian peasants carrying samovars are crying 'Hot *sbiten*!',* and the first steps are littered with rusty cannonballs, bombs, grapeshot and cast-iron cannon of various calibres. A little further on is a wide open space with huge wooden beams, gun carriages and sleeping soldiers lying about; there are horses, waggons, green field guns, ammunition chests and stacks of small arms; soldiers, sailors, officers, women, children and merchants are moving this way and that; carts loaded with hay, sacks or barrels pass by; here and there you will see a mounted Cossack or officer, or a general in his droshky. The street on the right is closed off by a barricade, with small cannon mounted in the embrasures and a sailor sitting beside them, puffing at his pipe.

---

* Spiced tea with honey.

To the left is a handsome house with Roman numerals carved into its pediment, beneath which some soldiers are standing beside bloodstained stretchers. Everywhere you see the unattractive features of a military encampment. Your first impression is bound to be most unpleasant: this odd mixture of camp life and town life, the beautiful city with a dirty bivouac, is more than unsightly—it looks a repulsive mess. You may even feel that everyone is in a panic, rushing hither and thither and not knowing what to do. But take a closer look at the faces of the people moving around you and you will realize that this is nothing of the sort. Just look at this convoy soldier leading his team of three bay horses to be watered—he's muttering so placidly to himself, he's clearly in no danger of losing his way in this motley crowd, which doesn't even exist for him. He just gets on with his job, whatever it may be—from watering horses to dragging a field gun—as coolly, calmly and confidently as if all this was happening somewhere in Tula or Saransk. And you'll see the same expression on the faces of the officer walking past in his immaculate white gloves, and the sailor sitting smoking on the barricade, and those soldiers in the working party waiting with their stretchers on the steps of what used to be the Assembly Hall, and that young lady skipping from stone to stone across the street, careful not to wet her pink dress.

Yes, you're bound to be disappointed if this is the first time you've entered Sevastopol. On all the faces you see, you'll search in vain for any sign of fuss or bother, or even of enthusiasm, determination or readiness to die—there's none of that. You see everyday people calmly going about their everyday business—you may even end up reproaching yourself for your own excessive fervour, and come to doubt some of that talk of the heroism of Sevastopol's defenders which has reached you through tales and descriptions of the sights and sounds on the North Side. But before giving way to such doubts, go down to the bastions, watch the defenders of Sevastopol on the defences themselves, or better still, walk across this very street and step into that building that used to be the Sevastopol Assembly, where the soldiers with their stretchers are standing on the steps—and you'll see the defenders of Sevastopol, and witness terrible and tragic sights, and noble and amusing ones—sights which will astonish you and fill your soul with exaltation.

You step inside and find yourself in the great Assembly Hall. As soon as you open the door, you are suddenly assailed by the sight and smell of some forty or fifty amputees and critically wounded men, some on camp beds but most lying on the floor. Ignore the feeling that makes you hesitate in the doorway—it's not a good feeling—but go on in, don't be ashamed that you appear to have come just to *look* at these sufferers, don't be ashamed to go up and chat to them. People who are in misery like seeing a sympathetic human face, they like talking about their sufferings and hearing words of love and compassion. You walk down between the beds, looking for a face less stern and less full of suffering, and make up your mind to approach and have a conversation.

'Where's your wound?' you ask shyly and tentatively, addressing a gaunt old soldier sitting on his camp bed, whose eyes are following you with a good-natured look as if inviting you to approach. I said you ask 'shyly', because as well as arousing your profound compassion, his suffering somehow also inspires you with a fear of causing offence, and with the deepest respect for the sufferer.

'My leg,' replies the soldier; and at that very moment you notice, from the folds in the blanket, that he has lost his leg above the knee. 'Thank God,' he adds, 'I'll get my discharge now.'

'Is it long since you were wounded?'

'Coming up six weeks, your Honour.'

'And does it still hurt now?'

'No, it doesn't hurt now, it's all right, only there's a sort of dragging ache in my calf when the weather's bad, that's all.'

'How did it happen?'

'On the fifth bastion, sir, in the first bombardment—I'd just trained a cannon and was walking away from it, like that, to another embrasure, when *he* got me in the leg—just as though I'd stepped into a hole. I looked, and my leg wasn't there.'

'Surely it must have hurt in that first moment?'

'Not too bad; only it felt as if they'd shoved something hot into my leg.'

'Well, but afterwards?'

'Afterwards it wasn't too bad either, except when they started stretching the skin over it, there was a scorching feeling. First thing is, your Honour, *not to think too much.* So long as you don't think about it, nothing matters. The worst is thinking about things.'

At this point a woman in a grey striped dress and a black kerchief comes up to you, joins in your conversation with the sailor and starts telling you all about him, and what he's suffered, and what a dreadful situation he was in for a whole four weeks, and how after he was wounded, he made the stretcher bearers stop to watch our battery firing a salvo, and how the grand dukes talked to him and gave him twenty-five roubles, and he told them that he wanted to get back to the bastion to instruct the young men if he wasn't fit to fight any more himself. Getting all this out in one breath, the woman glances at you and then at the sailor, who has turned away and seems not to be listening to her, but is picking at some lint on his pillow, and her eyes gleam with special intensity.

'That's my missis, your Honour,' the sailor remarks, with an expression that seems to say 'Don't mind her—you know what women are, talking a lot of nonsense.'

You're beginning to understand the defenders of Sevastopol; for some reason you're beginning to feel guilty in this man's presence. There's too much that you'd like to say to him, to express your sympathy and admiration; but you can't find the words, or you're dissatisfied with the ones that come into your head—so you say nothing, just bow your head before this man's mute, unconscious majesty and firmness of spirit, this modesty in the face of his own courage.

'Well, God grant you a quick recovery,' you say, and stop beside another invalid who is lying on the floor and appears to be in unbearable agony as he waits for death.

He is a fair-haired man, with a pale, swollen face, lying face upwards with his left arm flung out, in a posture that speaks of cruel suffering. His parched, open mouth is taking laboured, stertorous breaths; his blue, leaden eyes are rolled upwards, and his thrown-back blanket reveals the remains of his right arm, wrapped in bandages. You are assailed even more strongly by the oppressive smell of a dead body, and you yourself seem to be penetrated by the consuming inner fire that rages in every one of the victim's limbs.

'So is he unconscious?' you ask the woman, as she follows you around and gazes lovingly at you as if you were family.

'No, he can still hear, but he's very bad,' she whispers. 'I gave him some tea today—you can't help feeling sorry for him, even if he's one of theirs—but he hardly touched it.'

'How are you feeling?' you ask him.

He moves his eyes in response to your voice, but he neither sees nor understands you.

'Heart's on fire.'

A little further on you come to an old soldier changing his linen. His face and body are a sort of brownish colour, and thin as a skeleton's. One arm is completely missing, cut off at the shoulder. He's sitting straight up, wide awake; he has recovered from the operation. But his dull, deathly expression, his dreadful gaunt frame and heavily lined face tell you that this is a man at the close of a life full of suffering.

Lying on a bed on the other side of the room you see the pale, tortured and gentle face of a woman, with a hot, feverish flush covering her cheek.

'That's one of our sailors' wives, she was hit in the leg by a bomb on the 5th,' says your guide. 'She was carrying her husband's dinner to him on the bastion.'

'And so—did they amputate it?'

'Cut it off above the knee.'

Now, if you have strong nerves, go through the door on the left, to the room where they're doing dressings and carrying out operations. You'll see doctors there with pale faces and grim expressions, their arms covered in blood up to the elbows, working by a bed on which a chloroformed patient is lying open-eyed, deliriously mouthing meaningless words, or sometimes just simple and touching ones. The doctors are engaged in the repugnant but merciful work of amputation. You will see the sharp curved knife entering the healthy white flesh; you will see the wounded man suddenly regain consciousness, with a ghastly, harrowing scream and curses; you will see the assistant fling the severed arm into the corner; you will see another wounded man lying on a stretcher in the same room, watching his fellow soldier's operation, and writhing and groaning not so much from physical pain as from the psychological stress of waiting—you will see horrifying, blood-curdling sights, you will see war not in its fine, orderly and glorious aspect, with bands and drum rolls, fluttering banners and generals prancing along on horseback, but in its true essence, in its blood and suffering and death.

As you leave this house of pain, you cannot help feeling a sense of relief—you will take a deeper breath of fresh air, feel pleasure in the knowledge of your own good health, but at the same time, contemplating the suffering you have seen, you will find a sense of your own insignificance. And you will make your way, calmly and unhesitatingly, to the bastions.

'What can the death and suffering of a paltry worm like myself mean in the face of so many deaths and so much suffering?' you will ask yourself. But the sight of the clear sky, the brilliant sun, the handsome city, the open church and the soldiers moving this way and that, will soon restore your spirits to their normal condition of insouciance, trivial concerns and exclusive preoccupation with the present.

Perhaps you may encounter some officer's funeral procession emerging from the church, with a rose-coloured coffin, a band and flying banners; perhaps you will hear the sounds of firing coming from the bastions; but all this will not take you back to your previous thoughts. The funeral will strike you as a very fine military spectacle, and those sounds as very fine military sounds; you will not associate either the spectacle or the sounds with your own very clear personal thoughts about suffering and death, as you did at the dressing station.

Passing the church and the barricade, you enter the liveliest quarter of the city. Shop and inn signs line both sides of the street. The merchants, the women in their bonnets or headscarves, the smartly turned-out officers, all bear witness to the firm resolution, the self-confidence and security of the city's inhabitants.

If you want to hear the sailors and officers conversing, step into the inn on the right; they're sure to be talking about last night's doings, and the girl called Fenka, and the action on the 24th, and how bad and expensive the meatballs are in this place, and how this comrade and that one has been killed.

'It's just godawful where we are!' comes the deep voice of a yellow-haired, clean-shaven little sea officer in a knitted green scarf.

'Where's that?' someone else asks him.

'Fourth bastion,' says the young officer, and as soon as you hear the words 'fourth bastion', you can't help taking more notice of this fair-haired young officer and even viewing him with some respect. His exaggeratedly cool manner, the way he waves his arms about, his loud voice and laugh that you had found offensive, will now strike you as that special kind of devil-may-care bravado that some very young men affect after passing through danger. Now you're expecting to hear him telling you how terrible it is on the fourth bastion, from all the mortar bombs and bullets—but not a bit of it! It's the mud that's so terrible. 'You can't get across to the battery,' he says, pointing to his boots, which are caked knee-deep in mud.

'Well, they killed my best gunner today,' says someone else; 'got him right in the forehead.' — 'Who was that? Mityukhin?' — 'No... Hey, am I ever getting my veal? Lazy slobs!' he adds in the waiter's direction. 'No, not Mityukhin, it was Abrosimov. A great fellow, he was—he'd been in six sorties.'

Sitting at the other end of the table, over plates of meatballs with green peas and a bottle of that sour Crimean wine they call 'Bordeaux', are two infantry officers. One of them, a young man with a red collar and two stars on his greatcoat, is telling the other, an older man with a black collar and no stars, all about the battle of the Alma. The younger man has already drunk a fair amount, and his hesitancy as he tells his story, his uncertain air that betrays his doubts about whether he will be believed, and above all the improbably important part he seems to have played in the action, and how horrible it all was—all this makes it clear that he is taking great liberties with the actual truth. But you have no time for tales of this sort, which you will go on hearing in every corner of Russia for a long time to come. You want to hurry off to the bastions, and particularly the fourth, about which you have been hearing so many very different accounts. Whenever anyone announces that he was on the fourth bastion, he takes special pride and satisfaction in saying so; if anyone says 'I'm going to the fourth bastion', you will always detect a shadow of anxiety or too great a show of indifference; if a man wants to make fun of someone, he'll say 'They ought to send you to the fourth bastion'; and when people meet a stretcher and ask 'Where from?', the answer is usually 'The fourth bastion.' Generally speaking, there are two very different views going round about this terrible bastion. There are those who have never been there, and are convinced that the fourth bastion is a sure grave for anyone who ventures there; and those who live on it, like the little yellow-haired midshipman, who, if they mention the fourth bastion, will talk about whether it's dry or muddy, whether their dugout is warm or cold, and the like.

During the half-hour you've spent in the inn, the weather has changed—the sea mist that covered the water has gathered into gloomy, damp, grey clouds obscuring the sun, and a dreary drizzle is coming down, wetting the roofs, pavements and the soldiers' greatcoats...

Passing through another barricade, you emerge from a doorway on the right and walk up the main street. Beyond this barricade the houses on either side of the street are deserted, there are no shop signs, the doorways are boarded up, the windows knocked out; here the corner of a wall has been broken away, there a roof has been smashed in. The buildings look like old veterans who have lived through all kinds of woes and privations, and seem to be eyeing you with pride and a certain contempt. On your way you stumble over cannonballs scattered here and there, and trip over potholes full of water, carved out by shells falling on the stony ground. Along the street you meet or overtake groups of soldiers, Cossack scouts or officers; occasionally you encounter a woman or a child, but by now the woman won't be in a bonnet—she'll be a sailor's wife in an old fur cloak and army boots. Carrying on along the street and down a little slope, you find you are not among houses any more, but odd-looking piles of rubble, stones, boards, clay and beams; ahead of you, up a steep hill, you can see a black, muddy expanse criss-crossed by ditches, and what you're seeing out there is the actual fourth bastion... Here you meet even fewer people, there are no women to be seen, and the soldiers are hurrying along; you come across drops of blood on the road, and you are bound to meet four soldiers carrying a stretcher, and upon the stretcher a pale, yellowish face under a bloodstained greatcoat. If you ask 'Where's he wounded?' the stretcher bearers will answer you angrily, without turning towards you, to say it's in the leg or arm, if the wound is a slight one; or else keep a stony silence, if the head can't be seen on the stretcher and he's already dead or gravely wounded.

The whistle of a cannonball or mortar bomb close by, as you start climbing the hill, will give you an unpleasant shock. You will suddenly understand, in quite a different way from before, the real significance of those sounds of gunfire which you heard in the city. Some tranquil, happy memory will suddenly rise up in your imagination; you'll begin to take much more of an interest in your own person than in what you're seeing; you'll be less concerned with what is around you, and will succumb to a sudden feeling of hesitancy. But you ignore the cowardly voice that has suddenly begun to speak inside you at the sight of danger, and force it to be silent—particularly when you see a soldier running past you at a trot, laughing and waving his arms about as he slithers downhill through the wet mud. Instinctively you straighten out your chest, hold your head high and scramble on up the slippery clay slope. As soon as you've got a little higher, carbine bullets start whizzing past you from right and left, and you will perhaps wonder whether you had not better go on along the trench that runs parallel with the road; but the trench is filled higher than knee-deep with such stinking, liquid, yellow mud that you're bound to choose the road, particularly when you see everyone else doing the same. Some two hundred paces further on, you come to a ploughed-up expanse of mud surrounded by gabions, trenches and embankments, platforms and dugouts, with great cast-iron guns standing on them and neat piles of cannonballs beside them. All this seems to you to have been heaped up here without any sense, coherence or order. Here, sitting on the battery, is a group of sailors; there, in the middle of the open ground, half sunk into the mud, lies a broken cannon; there goes an infantryman carrying his musket across the battery, barely managing to pull his feet out of the clinging mud. But everywhere, on all sides, wherever you look, you see bomb splinters, unexploded bombs, cannonballs, the remnants of an encampment—and all of it sunk in the liquid, viscous mud. You seem to hear the thud of a cannonball falling nearby; on all sides you think you can hear every kind of bullet noises—buzzing like bees, whistling sharply past, or humming like a plucked string. You hear the dreadful boom of a cannon firing, which shakes you to the core and fills you with utter dread.

'So this is it, the fourth bastion; here it is, this awful, truly terrible place!' you think to yourself, with a little bit of pride and a very great deal of repressed terror. But you're in for a disappointment—this isn't the fourth bastion yet, it's only the Yazon redoubt, relatively pretty safe and not at all terrible. To get to the fourth bastion, you must turn to the right, along this narrow trench, where the infantryman went, keeping his head down. Here you may meet another stretcher, or a sailor, or soldiers with shovels; you may see mine cables, or dugouts in the mud with barely room for two men bent double. You'll see the Cossack scouts of the Black Sea battalions, changing their boots, eating, smoking their pipes, carrying on with their lives; and everywhere you'll see that same stinking mud, traces of encampments, and abandoned lumps of cast iron of every conceivable shape. Walk on another three hundred steps and you'll come to another battery, on an area of open ground crossed by trenches and covered by gabions covered in earth, cannon on platforms and earth embankments. Here you may see a group of four or five sailors playing cards in the shelter of the breastworks, and a naval officer who, observing that you're a new arrival and curious to know more, will take pleasure in showing off his domain and everything you might find interesting. This officer rolls his yellow paper cigarette so calmly, sitting on a cannon, and strolls so calmly from one embrasure to another, and chats so calmly to you, without the slightest affectation, that despite all the bullets whizzing past you, thicker than ever, you yourself come to feel cool-headed, question him attentively and listen to what he tells you. This officer will tell you—but only if you question him—about the bombardment on the 5th; he'll tell you how in his battery only one gun could be fired, and out of all his gunners there were only eight left, and how in spite of that, next day on the 6th he was firing from all his guns; he'll tell you about the bomb that landed on a sailors' dugout on the 5th and wiped out eleven men; he'll take you to an embrasure to show you the enemy batteries and trenches, no further than seventy or eighty yards away. But I'm afraid that you, encouraged by the whizzing bullets, may stick your head out of the embrasure to have a look at the enemy, and not see anything; or if you do see anything, you'll be very surprised to find that this white stone rampart, so close to you, with puffs of white smoke popping up from it—this same white rampart is the enemy, it's *him*, as the soldiers and sailors say.

And it's quite possible that this naval officer—either out of vanity or just for his own amusement—may decide to do some firing while you're there. 'Gunner and crew to the cannon!'—and some fourteen sailors hurry to the gun, brisk and lively, one of them tucking his pipe away in his pocket, another finishing his crust of dry bread. Clattering over the platform in their hobnailed boots, they come up to the gun and load it. Take a good look at these men's faces, their bearing and movements. Every crease of their weathered, high-cheekboned faces, every muscle, all those broad shoulders, all those stout legs in their enormous boots, every calm, confident, unhurried movement, all display those cardinal features that go to make up the Russian's strength: his stubborn, straightforward nature. But here you seem to see, on every face, how danger, bitterness and the suffering of war have added something more: a sense of their own dignity, and their lofty thoughts and feelings.

Suddenly you are engulfed in a terrible, shattering roar, which does not merely deafen your ears, but shakes you to the root of your being. Your whole body shudders. Next you hear the departing whistle of the cannonball, and a thick cloud of gunpowder smoke envelops you and the platform, and the black shapes of the sailors moving about on it. Following this shot from our battery, you will hear the sailors exchanging various opinions about it, you'll see how excited they are, and observe them expressing a feeling you may not have been expecting—a feeling of hatred for the enemy and thirst for revenge, which lurks in everyone's soul. 'Landed right in the embrasure—seems to have killed two of them… There, they're carrying them away,' you hear their delighted exclamations. 'Now he'll see red—he'll be chucking one over here in a minute,' someone says. And sure enough, a moment later you'll see a lightning flash and smoke out there; the sentry standing on the parapet yells 'Cannon!', then a cannonball shrieks past you and smacks into the ground, sending a column of dirt and stones into the air out of its crater. The battery commander will be very annoyed at this cannonball, and will order a second and third gun to be loaded; the enemy will respond, and you'll experience some interesting emotions, and hear and see some interesting things. The sentry will give another shout of 'Cannon!' and you'll hear the same shriek and impact, and the same shower of earth. Or else he'll shout 'Mortar!' and you'll hear the smooth whistle of a mortar bomb, quite a nice sound that is difficult to associate with anything very horrible; you'll hear that whistle coming closer and closer, moving faster and faster, then you'll see a black sphere coming down and striking the ground, and hear its ringing explosion, and feel it in your body. Bomb splinters hurtle past, whistling and screeching in all directions, stones fly through the air with a rushing sound, and you'll be spattered with mud. Hearing these noises, you'll experience a strange feeling of pleasurable enjoyment mixed with terror. At the instant when you know a bomb is flying towards you, you can't help thinking that the bomb is going to kill you; but your sense of self-respect sustains you, and no one else notices the knife that is tearing at your heart. And then, when the bomb has sailed past without touching you, you recover your spirits, and are overcome—but only for an instant—by an inexpressibly pleasant, cheerful sensation, so that you begin to discover a peculiar sort of charm in danger, in this game of life and death. You start wanting these cannonballs and bombs to fall closer to you, and even closer. But now the sentry's loud, rich voice has shouted 'Mortar!' once again, and there's another whistle, an impact and an explosion—but at the same time as the explosion you are suddenly aware of a man's groan. You go over to the wounded man, lying there covered in blood and dirt and looking somehow strange and unlike a human being; you reach him at the same time as the stretcher party. Part of the sailor's chest has been blown off. During these first moments, his mud-stained face registers nothing but alarm and the sort of feigned premature expression of suffering which one often sees on men in this situation. But as the stretcher is brought to him and he lies down on it on his good side, you notice that this expression is giving way to one of exaltation and some lofty, unspoken thought: his eyes gleam brighter, his teeth are clenched, his head rises higher with an effort; and as he is lifted up, he stops the stretcher and addresses his companions in a strained, tremulous voice: 'Sorry, lads!' He wants to say something else, obviously trying to say something moving, but all he can manage is to repeat the same words, 'Sorry, lads!' Now a fellow sailor comes up to him, puts the man's cap back on his head which he holds up for him, and walks back calmly and indifferently to his gun, swinging his arms as he goes. 'We get seven or eight like that every day,' the naval officer tells you, responding to the look of horror on your face; and he yawns and rolls another cigarette in yellow paper.

So now you have seen the defenders of Sevastopol on their actual lines of defence, and you make your way back, for some reason ignoring the cannonballs and bullets which still whistle round you all the way back to the ruined theatre. You walk in a state of calm exaltation. The chief reassuring conviction you come away with is that it is impossible for Sevastopol to be captured; and not only for Sevastopol to be captured, but for the strength of the Russian people to be shaken in any way, anywhere at all. You have seen this impossibility, not in the multitude of traverses, parapets, cunningly criss-crossing trenches, mines and cannon, positioned one behind the other, of which you have understood nothing—you have seen it in the eyes, the speech, the actions, in what is called the spirit, of the defenders of Sevastopol. Whatever they do, they do it so simply, with so little effort and exertion, that you are convinced they must be capable of a hundred times more—capable of anything. You realize that the feeling which motivates them is not the same as the petty, vain, unthinking emotions that you yourself have been experiencing, but a different sort of thing altogether, something more powerful, which has turned them into men capable of living just as calmly under cannon fire, with a hundred chances of death as compared with the one to which all of us are subject—and living under these conditions while subjected to ceaseless toil, sleeplessness and dirt. No one could tolerate such appalling conditions for the sake of a cross or a title, or in response to a threat; there must be some other, loftier motive. And that motive is a feeling that does not often show itself outwardly, one that Russians are shy of, but which they all cherish in their heart of hearts—love of their mother country. We know the stories of the early days of the siege of Sevastopol, when there were no fortifications, no troops, no physical possibility of holding it, and yet no one had the faintest doubt that it would never yield to the enemy. We know about Kornilov, that hero worthy of ancient Greece, and the time when he was reviewing his army and proclaimed: 'We'll die, boys, but we won't surrender Sevastopol!', and our Russian soldiers, not adept at high-sounding phrases, responded: 'We'll die! Hurrah!' But only now have the tales of those days ceased to be just a fine historical legend, and become reality, an observable fact. Now you will clearly realize that those men whom you have just seen are the very same heroes who in those hard times did not lose heart, but raised their spirits high, joyfully prepared to die not for a city but for their motherland. Long will this epic story of Sevastopol leave its mighty traces in Russia—a story whose hero was the Russian people.

Dusk is already falling. Just before sundown, the sun has emerged from the grey storm clouds that covered the sky, casting a sudden crimson glow over the purple thunderclouds, the grey-green sea dotted all over with ships and boats rocking on the broad, even swell, the white buildings of the city, and the people moving along the streets. Wafted over the water come the notes of an old waltz played by the regimental band on the boulevard, strangely echoed by the sounds of gunfire from the bastions.

Sevastopol, 25 April 1855

SEVASTOPOL IN MAY

1

SIX MONTHS HAVE already passed since the first cannonball whistled from the bastions of Sevastopol and ploughed up the earth on the enemy's earthworks, and since that time thousands of bombs, cannonballs and bullets have never stopped flying from the bastions into the trenches, and from the trenches onto the bastions, and the angel of death has never ceased to hover over them.

By now, thousands of personal vanities have been bruised, thousands have been satisfied and swollen up with pride, and thousands have found rest in the arms of death. How many medals and stars have been pinned on, how many ripped off, how many St Anne and St Vladimir ribbons awarded, how many pink coffins and cloth palls! But the same sounds still ring out from the bastions, and on a clear evening the French—full of instinctive trepidation and superstitious terror—still stare out from their encampments at the furrowed yellow earth of the Sevastopol bastions, the black figures of our sailors moving around on them, and count the embrasures with the cast-iron cannon poking angrily out of them; the petty-officer navigator still looks down through his telescope from the telegraph tower at the colourful figures of the French troops, their batteries, their tents, the columns moving on the Green Hill, the puffs of smoke rising from the trenches; and still the throngs of people from anywhere and everywhere, with all sorts of different aims and desires, and all driven by the same zeal as ever, continue to flock to this fatal place.

But the dispute which the diplomats have been unable to resolve is even less capable of being resolved by gunpowder and blood.

An odd thought has often occurred to me. Supposing one of the warring sides were to suggest to the other that a single soldier should be dismissed from each army? The idea might seem strange, but why not try it? Then dismiss a second one from each side, and a third and a fourth and so on, until each army was left with only a single soldier (assuming that the armies were of equal strength, and that quantity could be substituted by quality). And then, if it still appeared that complex political issues between rational representatives of rational political entities had to be resolved by a fight, let the fighting be done by those two soldiers, one besieging the city and the other defending it.

This argument may look paradoxical, but it is a sound one. For indeed, what would be the difference between one Russian fighting one representative of the allies, and eighty thousand fighting eighty thousand? Or why not a hundred and thirty-five thousand against a hundred and thirty-five thousand? Why not twenty thousand against twenty thousand? Or twenty men against twenty? So why not one against one? None of these figures is more logical than any other. Indeed, the last is the most logical, because it is more humane. There are only two ways about it: either war is madness, or, if men commit this madness, then they are not, as for some reason is generally supposed, rational beings at all.

2

IN THE BESIEGED CITY of Sevastopol, not far from the pavilion on the boulevard, a regimental band was playing, and crowds of soldiers, sailors and women were strolling along the paths in holiday mood. The bright spring sun had risen that morning over the English earthworks, moved on over the bastions and then the town, over the Nikolaevsky barracks, shining just as joyously over those too, and was now sinking down towards the distant blue sea, whose rhythmical rise and fall threw up glittering silver reflections.

A tall, slightly stooping infantry officer, pulling on a glove which, though not absolutely white, was still quite decent, emerged through the gate of one of the little sailors' houses that had been put up on the left side of Morskaya Street and set off up the hill towards the boulevard, gazing thoughtfully down at the ground. The expression on this officer's plain, low-browed face showed him to be rather dull-witted, but at the same time sober-minded, honest and upright. Physically he was rather ungainly—long-legged, awkwardly built and somehow diffident in his movements. He was wearing a new-looking cap, a thin greatcoat of a rather peculiar lilac shade with a gold watch chain peeping out at the breast, trousers with foot straps, and a pair of calfskin boots that were clean and shiny, but with heels that were rather worn in places. But it was not so much these items, not often seen on infantry officers, as the general effect of his whole person that would have immediately revealed to an experienced military man that this was not quite an ordinary infantry officer, but someone rather superior. He might have passed as a German, if his facial features had not made his purely Russian origins quite clear; or as an adjutant or regimental quartermaster (but then he would have been wearing spurs), or an officer transferred from the cavalry or even the Guards for the duration of the campaign. And he was indeed an ex-cavalryman. Just at the present moment, as he walked up towards the boulevard, he was thinking about a letter he had just received from a retired service comrade of his, a landowner in T—— province, and the man's wife, the pale, blue-eyed Natasha, his great friend. He was thinking of one particular passage in the letter, where his comrade had written:

'When they deliver *The Veteran*, Pupka' (this was what this retired Uhlan called his wife) 'rushes headlong into the hall, seizes the newspapers and runs off with them to the *S-shaped seat* in the *arbour*, which is to say the drawing room (in which, if you remember, we spent such delightful winter evenings with you when your regiment was stationed in our town), and reads about your heroic exploits with such excitement, you simply can't imagine. She often says of you: "Now Mikhailov, what an *absolute darling* he is, I'd like to cover him in kisses next time I see him; he's *fighting on the bastions*, and he's bound to get the St George Cross, and be written about in the papers," and so on and so forth, so much that I really begin to feel jealous of you.'

And in another place he had written: 'The newspapers only get here terribly late, and although we hear a lot of news by word of mouth, you can't believe all you hear. For instance, the *musical young ladies* you know of were telling us yesterday that Napoleon had been captured by our Cossacks and sent to Petersburg, but you can imagine how much of all that I believe. And one man who had arrived from Petersburg (he works on special assignments for a minister, a terribly nice man, and now that there's no one here in town, he's such a *risource* for us, you simply can't imagine),—well, he declares for a fact that our forces have taken Eupatoria, so the French *no longer have any contact with Balaklava*, and our side lost two hundred men killed in the action, while the French lost up to fifteen thousand. My wife was so thrilled with this that she *went on the spree* all night, and says she had a feeling that you must certainly have been in that action and distinguished yourself...'

In spite of the words and expressions I have purposely put in italics, and in spite of the whole tone of the letter, from which the disdainful reader will no doubt have reached a correctly unfavourable opinion of the respectability of Staff Captain Mikhailov himself, with his down-at-heel boots, and of his friend who writes about a *risource* and has such strange notions of geography, and of the staff captain's pale friend Natasha on the *S-shaped seat* (whom he may possibly and quite correctly imagine with dirty nails), and of the whole grubby, idle provincial *milieu* which he so despises—in spite of all this, Staff Captain Mikhailov was thinking back to his pale provincial friend with inexpressibly mournful fondness, remembering how he used to spend evenings sitting beside her in the arbour, talking about *feelings*. And he remembered, too, his good-natured comrade the Uhlan, and how he used to get so cross and end up having to pay forfeits when they played cards in his study for kopek stakes, and how his wife used to make fun of him. He remembered how fond of him those two people had been (and perhaps he felt there had even been something more on the part of his pale friend). Both these people, and all their home life, passed before his eyes, bathed in wonderfully sweet, happy, rosy colours. Smiling at his memories, he patted the pocket in which *that dear letter* rested. These memories were made even more precious to Staff Captain Mikhailov because the social circles in which he now moved, in his infantry regiment, were so much lower than those he used to frequent as a cavalry officer and a ladies' man, always well received in the town of T——.

The circles in which he used to move were so much more elevated than his present ones, that when in some moment of candour he found himself telling his infantry comrades how he used to drive his own droshky, or dance at the governor's balls and play cards with a general in the civil service, they would listen to him with a kind of sceptical indifference, as if they simply did not feel like contradicting him and proving him wrong; 'Let him talk,' they would think—and if he showed no obvious contempt for his comrades' binges, their vodka-swilling, their card games for kopek stakes with old cards, and the general coarseness of their lives, that must be put down to his particularly unassuming, respectful and sensible character.

From these recollections Staff Captain Mikhailov found himself passing on to his hopes and dreams. 'How surprised and delighted Natasha will be,' he thought, striding along a narrow lane in his down-at-heel boots, 'when she suddenly finds a description in *The Veteran* of me being the first to climb up on the cannon, and getting the St George Cross. And they'll have to promote me to full captain by virtue of my seniority. Then it's quite likely they'll make me a major of the line, because so many officers have been killed; and probably a great many more of us will be killed in this campaign. And then there'll be another action, and as a distinguished man, they'll give me a regiment... I'll be a lieutenant-colonel... the St Anne ribbon round my neck... colonel...' and in no time he was a general, condescending to visit Natasha, his comrade's widow—for in his dreams his friend was already dead—when the sounds of the regimental band broke into his reverie, crowds of people filled his gaze, and he found himself back on the boulevard, still a staff captain as ever, shy, awkward and insignificant.

3

FIRST HE WENT to the pavilion beside which the bandsmen were performing. Instead of music stands, they had other soldiers from their regiment holding their sheets of music open for them; and standing in a circle round them all, watching them rather than listening, were clerks, cadets, nannies with children, and officers in old greatcoats. Most of the people standing, sitting or strolling round the pavilion were either naval officers, adjutants or army officers in white gloves and new greatcoats. And along the broad avenue of the boulevard, all sorts of officers were walking up and down with all sorts of women, some of them in bonnets, most of them wearing kerchiefs, but some without either; the remarkable thing was that not one of them was old, they were all young women. Lower down, in the fragrant shady avenues of white acacias, separate groups sat or wandered around.

No one was particularly pleased to meet Staff Captain Mikhailov on the boulevard, except perhaps for Captains Obzhogov and Suslikov from his own regiment. Both of them shook his hand warmly—but the former was wearing camel-hair trousers and no gloves, he had a threadbare greatcoat and a red, perspiring face, while the latter talked at the top of his voice, and in such a familiar manner that Staff Captain Mikhailov felt embarrassed to be seen with them, particularly in front of officers in white gloves. He had exchanged bows with one of these officers, an adjutant, and could have exchanged bows with another as well—a staff officer—because he had met him twice before at the house of a mutual acquaintance. Besides, what was the attraction of strolling with these gentlemen, Obzhogov and Suslikov, when he anyway met them and shook hands with them half a dozen times a day? It was not for this that he had come to *listen to the band.*

He would have liked to go up to the adjutant whom he had greeted, and have a talk with those gentlemen—not at all so that Captains Obzhogov and Suslikov, and Lieutenant Pashtetsky and the rest, should see him talking to them, but simply because they were nice people, and knew all the latest news, and might pass some on…

But what is making Staff Captain Mikhailov so shy, unable to make up his mind to approach them? 'Supposing they decide not to return my greeting?' he is wondering. 'Or bow to me but carry on talking to each other as if I wasn't there? Or just walk away and leave me there all on my own, among the *aristocrats*?' The word *aristocrats*, in the sense of the highest elite group in any walk of life, has for some time now been extremely popular here in Russia, where one would have thought it really ought not to have existed at all. It has found its way into every corner of the country, and every level of society to which vanity has access (and where is the epoch or condition of society to which this repulsive little vice has not penetrated?)—among merchants, civil servants, clerks, officers, in Saratov, Mamadysh, Vinnitsa, anywhere where there are people. And since there are many people in the besieged city of Sevastopol, it follows that there is a great deal of vanity there too; in other words there are *aristocrats*, even though death hangs over the heads of every *aristocrat* and *non-aristocrat* alike, every minute of the day.

For Captain Obzhogov, Staff Captain Mikhailov is an *aristocrat*, because of his clean greatcoat and gloves, and so he hates him, although he also has a little respect for him. For Staff Captain Mikhailov, Adjutant Kalugin is an *aristocrat*, because he is an adjutant and on first-name terms with another adjutant; and hence Mikhailov is not entirely well disposed towards him, though afraid of him. For Adjutant Kalugin, Count Nordov is an *aristocrat*, and he constantly curses and despises him in his heart because he is an aide-de-camp to the Tsar. It's a terrible word, *aristocrat*. Why does Second Lieutenant Zobov utter such a forced laugh, even though there is nothing funny about it, when he passes by his companion who is sitting there with a staff officer? It's to prove that although he's no *aristocrat* himself, he's not a whit worse than them. Why is the staff officer talking in such a faint, wanly downcast and affected voice? In order to demonstrate to the other man that he is an *aristocrat* and is being extremely gracious by condescending to talk to a second lieutenant. Why is this officer cadet waving his arms about and winking like that, as he follows behind a lady whom he has never met before and would never dare accost? To demonstrate to all the officers that although he doffs his cap to them, he's an *aristocrat* just the same, and is having a great time. Why was the artillery captain so rude to the good-natured orderly? To prove to all and sundry that he never curries favour and has no need of *aristocrats*. And so on, and so on, and on.

Vanity, vanity, all is vanity—even on the brink of the grave, and among people ready to die for the sake of their exalted convictions. Vanity! It must be the defining characteristic of our age, its peculiar malady. Why had people in past ages never heard of this passion, any more than they had heard of smallpox or cholera? Why, in our own time, are there only three classes of people: those who accept the principle of vanity as an inescapable fact, and consequently a just one, to which they freely submit; those who accept it as an unfortunate but insuperable condition of life; and those, finally, who slavishly and unconsciously act under its influence? Why did Homer and Shakespeare and men like them speak of love, glory and suffering, while the literature of our own age has nothing but interminable accounts like *The Book of Snobs* and *Vanity Fair*?

Staff Captain Mikhailov twice walked past the group of his *aristocrats* without the courage to approach them, but on his third attempt he braced himself and went over to them. This group consisted of four officers: Adjutant Kalugin, whom Mikhailov knew; Adjutant Prince Galtsin, who was a bit of an aristocrat even for Kalugin; Lieutenant-Colonel Neferdov, one of the so-called 'Hundred and Twenty-two' society men who had come out of retirement and entered active service, partly out of patriotism, partly out of ambition, and mainly because everyone else was doing it; an old bachelor and Moscow clubman who had here joined the clique of malcontents who did nothing, understood nothing, and condemned every decision the authorities made; and finally, Cavalry Captain Praskukhin, another of the 'Hundred and Twenty-two' heroes. Fortunately for Mikhailov, Kalugin was in excellent spirits (he had just had a very confidential chat with the general, and Prince Galtsin, newly arrived from Petersburg, was putting up in his quarters), and did not consider it beneath him to shake hands with Staff Captain Mikhailov. This was more than Praskukhin could bring himself to do, however, though he had often run across Mikhailov on the bastion, had several times drunk his wine and vodka, and even owed him twelve and a half roubles from a game of preference. Not yet being well acquainted with Prince Galtsin, he preferred not to reveal his acquaintance with a plain infantry staff captain. He gave a slight bow in Mikhailov's direction.

'So, Captain,' said Kalugin, 'when are you off to the bastion again? Remember how we met on the Schwartz redoubt? Pretty hot, wasn't it?'

'Certainly was,' answered Mikhailov, ruefully remembering what a pathetic figure he had made that night, picking his way along the trench to the bastion, bent double, when he met Kalugin striding along in such a spirited way, carelessly rattling his sword.

'I'm actually supposed to go there tomorrow, but we've a man sick,' Mikhailov went on, 'one of the officers, so…' He wanted to explain that it wasn't his turn, but as the officer commanding No. 8 company was ill, and the only other officer left was a lieutenant, he had felt it his duty to offer to go instead of Lieutenant Nieprzysiecki, and so would be going to the bastion tonight. But Kalugin did not wait for him to finish.

'I have the feeling something's about to happen soon,' he said to Prince Galtsin.

'But won't there be something happening tonight?' Mikhailov asked timidly, looking from Kalugin to Galtsin and back again. No one answered him. Prince Galtsin merely frowned a bit, gazed out somewhere beyond Mikhailov's cap, and after a short silence, said:

'That's a pretty girl over there, in the red kerchief. Do you know her by any chance, Captain?'

'She's the daughter of a sailor who lives near my quarters,' replied the staff captain.

'Let's go and take a proper look at her.'

And Prince Galtsin took Kalugin's arm on one side and the staff captain's on the other, knowing full well in advance that this could not fail to give great pleasure to the latter, which was indeed the case.

The staff captain was superstitious, and regarded it as very sinful to have anything to do with women before an action; but on this occasion he pretended to be a great libertine—though evidently neither Prince Galtsin nor Kalugin believed him, while the girl in the red kerchief was quite astonished at him, having several times noticed him blushing as he walked past her window. Praskukhin followed behind them and kept nudging Prince Galtsin's arm and making various remarks in French; but as there was no room for all four of them to walk abreast along the path, he was forced to follow behind them on his own. It was only on their second circuit of the path that he managed to take the arm of Servyagin, a naval officer known for his bravery, who had come up to them because he too wanted to join the group of *aristocrats*. And the famous hero was delighted to thrust his honest, muscular arm under Praskukhin's elbow, though everyone, including Servyagin himself, knew that he was not a very good man. But when Praskukhin explained to Prince Galtsin how he knew this seaman, and whispered that he was a famous hero, Prince Galtsin (who had been on the fourth bastion last night and seen a bomb explode twenty paces away, and consequently felt no less a hero than this gentleman), decided that a great many reputations were gained for nothing much, and completely ignored Servyagin.

Staff Captain Mikhailov was so enjoying walking with these people that he quite forgot the *dear letter* from T——, and the dark thoughts he had been having at the prospect of having to go off to the bastion, and most importantly the fact that he had to be back in his quarters by seven o'clock. He stayed with the officers until they began to talk exclusively to one another and avoid his eye, making it clear that he might leave, and eventually walked off and left him. But Staff Captain Mikhailov was still quite satisfied, and as he walked past Baron Pest, a cadet who had been so full of conceit ever since spending the previous night in a dugout on the fifth bastion that he now felt he was a hero, Mikhailov was not in the least offended by the haughty and suspicious expression on the cadet's face as he stood to attention and doffed his cap.

4

BUT AS SOON as the staff captain crossed the threshold of his quarters, his head was filled with very different thoughts. He saw his little room with its uneven floor of packed earth and its crooked windows stuck over with paper, his old bed with a piece of carpet nailed to the wall above it depicting a lady on horseback, and a pair of Tula pistols hanging above that; and the dirty couch of the cadet who shared his lodging, with its cotton print coverlet. And he saw his manservant Nikita, scratching his tangled, greasy hair as he got up from the floor; and his ancient greatcoat, and civilian boots, and a little bundle with a lump of soapy cheese and the neck of a porter bottle filled with vodka poking out of it—the rations prepared for him to take to the bastion. And with a sense of something like dread he suddenly remembered that he had to take his company out this very evening to spend the whole night in the lodgements.

'I expect I'll get killed tonight,' thought the staff captain. 'I can feel it. And the worst of it is, I didn't need to go, I actually volunteered. And it's always the ones who volunteer that get killed. What's wrong with that damned Nieprzysiecki? As like as not, he's not ill at all, but here's a man who'll get killed because of him—sure as fate. Though actually, if I don't get killed, they're bound to promote me. I saw how pleased the regimental commander was when I said, let me go if Lieutenant Nieprzysiecki is ill. If they don't make me up to major, I'll certainly get the Vladimir

Cross. I mean, this will be my thirteenth time on the bastion. Oh dear! Thirteen, an unlucky number. I'll definitely be killed, I can feel it coming, I know I will. But someone had to go, you can't send a company out with no one but an ensign in command, something bad would have happened, it's the regiment's honour at stake here, the whole army's honour. It was my duty to go… yes, my duty. But I've got this premonition.' The staff captain was forgetting that this very same premonition came to him, more or less severely, every time he had to go out to the bastion; nor did he realize that the same premonition, more or less severe, comes to anyone who is about to go into action.

Somewhat reassured by this notion of duty, which—like all persons of limited intellect—the staff captain possessed to a powerful and highly developed degree, he sat down at the table and began writing a farewell letter to his father, with whom he had recently been on rather strained terms on account of money matters. Ten minutes later, when he had finished the letter, he got up from the table, his eyes wet with tears, and reciting in his head all the prayers he knew (for he was too embarrassed to pray aloud to God in his servant's presence), he began getting dressed. He would have very much liked to kiss the little icon of St Metrophanes which his late mother had given him with her blessing, and in which he particularly believed; but he was too embarrassed to do this in front of Nikita, so he brought his icons out of his frock coat in such a way that he could get at them without unbuttoning once he was in the street. His coarse, drunken servant listlessly handed him his new frock coat; the old one, which the staff captain generally wore when going out to the bastion, had not been mended.

'Why isn't the frock coat mended? All you ever do is sleep, you wretch!' said Mikhailov angrily.

'What d'you mean, sleep?' grumbled Nikita. 'Day in, day out, I'm running around like a dog, can't help getting tired—but still I'm not supposed to sleep.'

'You're drunk again, I see.'

'Not on your money, so don't go on at me.'

'Silence, you animal!' yelled the staff captain, on the point of striking him. He had been exasperated before, but now he had completely lost his temper, outraged by Nikita's rudeness—though he was actually fond of him, even spoilt him, and by now had lived with him for twelve whole years.

'Animal! Animal!' the servant repeated. 'What are you calling me an animal for, sir? Think of the times we live in. It's no time to be cursing and swearing.'

Mikhailov remembered where he was going, and felt ashamed.

'You'd put anyone out of temper with you, Nikita,' he said meekly. 'That letter's to my father, leave it where it is on the table and don't touch it,' he added, blushing.

'Yes, sir,' said Nikita, turned maudlin from the vodka he had drunk 'on his own money', as he said, and blinking his eyes in an attempt to make tears come.

But once the staff captain was out on the porch and said 'Goodbye, Nikita!', Nikita suddenly broke down in a paroxysm of forced sobs, and ran to kiss his master's hands. 'Farewell, master!' he snivelled through his tears.

The old sailor's widow was standing on the porch too, and as a woman she could not fail to join in this touching scene. She began wiping her eyes with her grubby sleeve and mumbling something about how even the gentry had their troubles to bear, and how she herself, poor woman, had been left a widow; and proceeded to tell drunken Nikita, for the hundredth time, about her own woes, and how her husband had been killed in the first bombardment, and her little home smashed to bits (the house where she now lived did not belong to her), and so on and so forth. When his master was gone, Nikita lit his pipe, asked the landlady's daughter to go and fetch some vodka, and very quickly stopped weeping—in fact he got into a quarrel with the old woman about a pail of his he said she had crushed.

'But perhaps I'll only be wounded,' the staff captain thought to himself, drawing near the bastion at dusk with his company of soldiers. 'But where? What'll it be like? Here? Or here?' he wondered, mentally pointing to his stomach and his chest. 'If it could just get me here,' he thought, meaning his upper thigh, 'it might only graze me. Yes, but if a splinter gets me there, I'm done for!'

However, the staff captain bent over double to get along the trenches, and managed to reach the lodgements unharmed. Here, by now in total darkness, he helped a sapper officer to detail the men off to their tasks, and then got down into a dugout below the parapet. There was not much gunfire; just now and then there would be a lightning flash from our side or *his*, and the glowing fuse of a mortar bomb would trace its fiery arc against the dark starry sky. But all the bombs were falling far to the rear on the right of the lodgement where the staff captain sat crouching in his dugout. Somewhat reassured, he swigged some vodka, ate a mouthful of soapy cheese, lit a cigarette, said a prayer and tried to get some sleep.

5

PRINCE GALTSIN, Lieutenant-Colonel Neferdov, Cadet Baron Pest (who had met them on the boulevard), and Praskukhin, whom no one had invited to join them, and to whom no one spoke, but who still trailed along behind them, all walked off from the boulevard to have tea with Kalugin.

'So, you never finished telling me about Vaska Mendel,' said Kalugin, when he had taken off his greatcoat and seated himself by the window on a soft, comfortable armchair, while unbuttoning the collar of his clean, starched Holland shirt. 'How did he get married?'

'You'll die laughing, my dear fellow! *Je vous dis, il y avait un temps où on ne parlait que de ça à Pétersbourg*,'* laughed Prince Galtsin, jumping up from the piano stool and sitting down on the windowsill next to Kalugin. 'You'll die laughing. I know all about it.' And with great wit, humour and style, he launched into an account of some love affair, which we will pass over since it is of no interest to us.

But the remarkable thing was that not only Prince Galtsin but all these gentlemen, once they had arranged themselves on the windowsill, or were sitting back with their legs drawn up, or by the piano, seemed to be quite different people from those they

---

* 'I tell you, there was a time when no one in Petersburg talked about anything else.'

had been on the boulevard. They had shed that absurd, pompous, haughty air which they affected in front of infantry officers; now they were among their own kind and behaved naturally, like very charming, high-spirited and agreeable fellows—especially Kalugin and Prince Galtsin. They were talking about their fellow officers and acquaintances in Petersburg.

'How's Maslovsky getting on?'

'Which one? The one in the Leib-Uhlans or in the Horse Guards?'

'I know them both. I knew the one in the Horse Guards when he was a boy, fresh out of school. What about the older one? Is he a captain yet?'

'Oh, ages ago!'

'Still carrying on with that Gipsy girl of his?'

'No, he dropped her.' And so on in the same strain.

Then Prince Galtsin sat down at the piano and gave a fine rendering of a Gipsy song. Praskukhin joined in to sing a second part, though no one had asked him, and did it so well that he was actually asked to go on. He was delighted.

The servant came in with tea, cream, and pretzels on a silver tray.

'Serve the prince,' said Kalugin.

'It's a strange thought, isn't it?' said Galtsin, taking his glass over to the window. 'Here we are in a besieged city, strumming on a piano, having tea with cream, in the sort of quarters I wish I had back in Petersburg.'

'Well, if we didn't even have that,' said the old lieutenant-colonel, always grumpy about everything, 'think how unbearable it would be, this everlasting waiting for something to happen… seeing men being killed, on and on, day after day, with no end to it—if we had to live up to our necks in the mud, with none of the comforts of life.'

'How about our infantry officers, then,' said Kalugin, 'living on the bastions alongside the soldiers, hiding in their dugouts and eating the same borsch as the men… What's it like for them?'

'Now that's something I don't understand, and I must confess I can't believe it,' said Galtsin. 'I don't see how men in dirty underwear, riddled with lice and with unwashed hands, can manage to be brave. You know, with *cette belle bravoure de gentilhomme…** It just isn't possible.'

'But they don't even understand that kind of bravery,' said Praskukhin.

'Don't talk such nonsense,' Kalugin interrupted crossly. 'I've seen more of these men than you have, and I'll tell you one thing. Our infantry officers, for all that they're louse-ridden and can't change their underwear for ten days on end—they're heroes, amazing people, and I don't mind who hears me say so.'

At this point an infantry officer entered the room.

'I'm… I've orders… Can I speak to Gen— to his Excellency, a message from General X?' he asked, with an embarrassed bow.

Kalugin got to his feet without returning the officer's bow, and with insulting courtesy and a forced official smile asked him to wait a moment. Then, without inviting the officer to sit down, and paying him no further attention, he turned to Galtsin and addressed him in French, leaving the unfortunate officer standing in the middle of the room, with no idea what to do with himself, or with his ungloved hands which were hanging down in front of him.

'It's on a very urgent matter, sir,' said this officer after a silence.

'Oh? Come along, then,' said Kalugin with the same insulting smile, putting on his greatcoat and escorting the man to the door.

---

* 'that fine gallantry of a gentleman'

'*Eh bien, messieurs, je crois que cela chauffera cette nuit,*'* said Kalugin when he emerged from the general's quarters.

'Oh? Why? What...? A sortie?' they all asked.

'I've no idea. Wait and see,' Kalugin answered with a cryptic smile.

'No, go on, do tell me,' said Baron Pest. 'If something's going to happen, I have to go with the T—— regiment on the first sortie.'

'Off you go then, and God bless you.'

'My boss is on the bastion too, so I suppose I've got to go as well,' said Praskukhin, buckling on his sword. But no one replied—it was up to him to know whether he had to go or not.

'Nothing's going to happen, I can tell,' said Baron Pest with a sinking heart as he contemplated the forthcoming action. But he still clapped on his cap at a rakish angle and strode out of the room with firm, noisy steps, together with Praskukhin and Neferdov who were also hurrying to their posts, weighed down by fear. 'Goodbye, gentlemen!' — 'Goodbye, gentlemen, I'll see you later on tonight!' Kalugin shouted out of the window, as Praskukhin and Pest, bending forward over the pommels of their Cossack saddles and no doubt imagining they were real Cossacks, trotted off down the road.

'Yes, a bit!' Pest shouted back, not having heard what Kalugin had said. And the clatter of the small Cossack horses' hooves soon died away down the dark street.

'*Non, dites-moi, est-ce qu'il y aura véritablement quelque chose cette nuit?*'† asked Galtsin, leaning over the windowsill with Kalugin and watching the mortar bombs rising and falling over the bastions.

* 'Well, gentlemen, I believe things are going to heat up tonight.'

† 'No, tell me, is something really going to be happening tonight?'

'I suppose I can tell you, see, because you've been on the bastions, haven't you?' (Galtsin nodded, although he had only once been on the fourth bastion.) 'Well, there was a trench facing our lunette...'—and Kalugin, who had no special knowledge although he fancied himself as a very good judge in military matters, began describing the dispositions of our earthworks and the enemy's, and the plan for the proposed action, but got rather muddled, mixing up the technical terms for the various fortifications.

'Oh look, their shots are landing near our lodgements now. Oho! Was that one of ours, or *his*? There, it's exploded!' they said, leaning on the windowsill and watching the fiery trails of the mortar bombs criss-crossing the sky, and the lightning flashes of gunshots that momentarily lit up the dark-blue sky, and the white gunpowder smoke, while they listened to the ever-intensifying sounds of gunfire.

'*Quel charmant coup d'œil!** Eh?' said Kalugin, drawing his guest's attention to the spectacle, which really was beautiful. 'You know, sometimes you can't tell the stars and the bombs apart.'

'Yes, I was just thinking that something was a star, but then it fell and exploded. And that big star—what's it called?—looks just like a bomb.'

'You know, I've got so used to these bombs, I'm sure that when I'm in Russia on a starry night, I'll have the impression that they're all bombs. You get so used to them.'

'What do you think, should I go out on this sortie?' Prince Galtsin said after a brief silence, shuddering at the mere thought of being out there during this terrifying cannonade, and reflecting with sweet relief that no one could possibly send him out there at night.

---

* 'What a charming sight!'

'Stop it, my lad! Don't even think of it. Anyway, I wouldn't let you go,' replied Kalugin, who knew very well that nothing would persuade Galtsin to go out there. 'Time enough, old chap!'

'Really? You don't think I ought to go? Eh?'

At that moment a terrible rattle of small-arms fire could be heard above the booming of the artillery, right in the direction these officers were looking, and thousands of little flashes shone out and kept reappearing, all along the line.

'Look, it's getting serious now!' said Kalugin. 'I can never hear that sound of small-arms fire without getting worked up—you know, somehow it gets you here. And now they're shouting "hurrah!",' he added, listening to the distant drawn-out roar of hundreds of voices: 'a-a-a-a-ah!' that was carried towards them from the bastion.

'Who's shouting "hurrah"? Them or us?'

'I don't know, but now they've started fighting hand-to-hand, because the firing's stopped.'

At this point an orderly officer escorted by a Cossack came galloping up to the porch by their window and dismounted.

'Where are you from?'

'The bastion. I need the general.'

'Come along. What's up?'

'They attacked the lodgements… took them… the French brought up huge reserves… attacked our forces… we only had two battalions,' panted the officer—the same one who had been there earlier in the evening. Hardly able to catch his breath, he still strolled over to the door in a thoroughly casual way.

'So have ours retreated?' asked Galtsin.

'No,' the officer answered crossly. 'Another battalion arrived and beat them off, but the regimental commander was killed, and lots of other officers too. My orders are to request reinforcements…'

With these words, he and Kalugin went in to see the general; and we will not follow them any further.

Five minutes later Kalugin had mounted his Cossack horse—again adopting that special quasi-Cossack posture which, as I have observed, all adjutants for some reason seem to find particularly attractive—and was setting off at a trot for the bastion to pass on some orders and wait for more news of the final outcome of the action. Meanwhile Prince Galtsin, succumbing to the painful excitement that generally overcomes those who observe a battle at close quarters but are not taking part in it, went out into the street and began to walk aimlessly up and down.

6

CROWDS OF SOLDIERS were carrying wounded men on stretchers or helping them along by their arms. The street was pitch dark; very occasionally, here and there, a light could be seen in a hospital window or in the quarters of some officers sitting up late. The same rumble of artillery and gunfire was still carried over from the bastions, and the same flashes of light still burst out against the black sky. From time to time, hoof beats would be heard as some orderly galloped by, or a wounded man's groan, the talk and footsteps of stretcher bearers, or the voices of frightened women when people came out onto the porch to watch the cannonade.

Among these were our old friend Nikita, and the old sailor's widow with whom he had already made his peace, and her ten-year-old daughter.

'Oh Lord, holy mother of God!' the old woman was muttering and sighing to herself as she watched the shells incessantly flying from one side or the other, like balls of fire. 'What horrors they are, such horrors! Ai-ai-ai-ai! There hasn't been anything like this, even in the first bombardment. Look up there, it's exploded, the wicked thing—right on top of our house outside the town.'

'No, it's further away, it's Aunty Irina's garden they keep falling in.'

'But where and oh where is my master right now?' Nikita intoned in a sing-song voice, still rather drunk. 'How I love that master of mine, more than I can say. He thrashes me, but I'm still that fond of him, something dreadful. Love him so much, if God forbid they kill him, such a sinful thing it would be, believe me, auntie, I just don't know what I'd do with myself, honest I don't! Such a master he is, there's no words for him! How could I change him for them there, playing at cards—they're just—ugh! No, there's no words for him!' concluded Nikita, pointing at his master's lighted window, where, in the staff captain's absence, the Polish cadet Żwadczeski had invited his friends over to help him celebrate the military cross he had just been awarded. His guests were Second Lieutenant Ugrowicz and Lieutenant Nieprzysiecki, the same man who was supposed to report to the bastion that evening but was off sick with a gumboil.

'Look at the stars, the stars are just tumbling down!' said the little girl, looking up at the sky and breaking the silence that had followed Nikita's words. 'There, there's another one fallen! What's it all for, hey, Mama?'

'Our little house'll be smashed to bits,' said the old woman with a sigh, leaving her daughter's question unanswered.

'And Mama, when Uncle and I were on our way there today,' the little girl went on in her sing-song voice, 'there was a huge, enormous cannonball lying right there in the room, next to the cupboard—it must have smashed through into the hallway and come flying into the room. Such a huge one it was, no one could have lifted it.'

'All the ones that had husbands and money, they all left,' said the old woman. 'But us, oh what a misery, what a misery, the only house we had, and they've blown it to pieces. Look at him, look at him firing, the fiend! Oh Lord, Lord!'

'And just as we were going to le-e-eave, another bomb came flying over and burst into pie-e-eces, and all the earth came scre-e-eaming through the air all over us, and a splinter nearly hit Uncle and me.'

'She ought to get a medal for that,' said the cadet, who had come out onto the porch with the officers to watch the exchange of fire.

'You go along and see the general, old lady,' said Lieutenant Nieprzysiecki, patting her on the shoulder. 'I mean it!'

'*Pójdę na ulicę zobaczyć, co tam nowego*,'* he added, going down the steps.

'*A my tym czasem napijmy się wódki, bo coś dusza w pięty ucieka*,'† Żwadczeski laughed merrily.

* 'I'll go out into the street to see what's new.'

† 'And meanwhile I'll have a nip of vodka, because my heart's sunk down into my boots.'

7

PRINCE GALTSIN met more and more wounded men, some on stretchers, others on foot being helped along by their fellows, and all talking loudly together.

'Never seen anything like it, boys,' one tall soldier was saying in a deep voice, as he trudged along with two guns over his shoulder. 'Leaping out at us, yelling "Allah, Allah!"* and all climbing over each other. You shoot one down, and the others just step over him—there's nothing you can do. Thousands of them, there were, all coming at once!'

At this point in his account, Galtsin stopped him.

'You've come from the bastion, have you?'

'Yes, your Honour.'

'Well, tell me, what happened there?'

'What happened? He sent a *force* up, and they came straight over the rampart, and that was the end of it. They smashed us to bits, your Honour!'

'What do you mean, smashed you? You beat them off, didn't you?'

'How could we beat them off, when *he* sent his whole *force* against us? Slaughtered all our men, and we didn't get any reinforcements.'

---

* In their battles with the Turks our soldiers have become so used to hearing this cry from their enemies that they now invariably maintain that the French cry 'Allah!' too. [*Note by Tolstoy*]

(The soldier was mistaken—the trench was still in Russian hands. But this is a peculiar feature that we can all observe: a soldier wounded in action always reckons that the action was lost, and that it was a dreadfully bloody one.)

'How is it I was told they'd been beaten off?' Galtsin demanded, in some annoyance.

At this point Lieutenant Nieprzysiecki came up, having recognized Prince Galtsin by his white cap, and anxious to take advantage of this chance to talk with such an important personage.

'Do you happen to know what went on up there, sir?' he asked respectfully, touching his cap.

'I'm just trying to discover,' said Prince Galtsin, and turned back to the soldier with the two guns. 'Perhaps they beat them off after you'd gone? How long is it since you left there?'

'Just now, your Honour!' said the soldier. 'It's not likely—they must have taken the trench. Beat us hollow, they did.'

'Well, shame on you, giving up a trench to the enemy! That's disgraceful!' said Galtsin, irritated by the soldier's apparent indifference. 'You should be ashamed of yourselves!' he repeated, turning away from him.

'Oh, these men are terrible! You don't know them, sir,' Lieutenant Nieprzysiecki echoed him. 'Let me tell you, you can't expect to see any pride, or patriotism, or proper feelings in these people. Just take a look, sir—all these crowds pouring in, there can't be one in ten of them that's wounded, the rest are all "helpers", all they want is to get away from the action. What a despicable lot! Shame on you, men, shame on you! Surrendering our trench like that!' he added, addressing the soldiers.

'What do you expect, when they sent a *force* over!' muttered the soldier.

'Eh, your Honour!' a soldier spoke up from the stretcher that was carrying him, as it came level with the lieutenant. 'How could we help giving it up, when almost every one of us had been killed? If we'd been there in *force*, we'd never have given it up, never in our lives. But what can you do? I got one of them with my bayonet, but then something hit me… Oh-oh, easy now, boys, go steady, boys—steady, I say… Oh-oh-oh!' the wounded man groaned.

'Right enough, it does look as if too many men are coming back,' said Galtsin, and stopped the same tall soldier with the two guns again. 'Why are you on your way back? Hey you, halt!'

The soldier halted and took off his cap with his left hand.

'Where are you off to, and what for?' the lieutenant shouted sternly. 'Good-for-no—'

But at that moment, coming right up to the soldier, he noticed that his right arm was tucked inside his coat, and soaked in blood well above the elbow.

'Wounded, your Honour!'

'How were you wounded?'

'Here, sir—must have been a bullet,' said the soldier, indicating his arm. 'And here, I've no idea what got me in the head,' and bending his head forward, he showed the bloody matted hair on the back of his head.

'Where did you get the other gun?'

'It's a French carbine, your Honour—I got it off him. And I wouldn't be here, only I had to see to this young fellow, or he'd have been falling over every step of the way,' he added, pointing to another soldier walking a little way ahead of him, leaning on his gun and dragging his left leg with an effort.

'And where are you off to, you scum!' yelled Lieutenant Nieprzysiecki at another soldier he ran into, hoping to impress the important prince with this show of zeal. That soldier also turned out to have been wounded.

Prince Galtsin suddenly felt terribly ashamed of Lieutenant Nieprzysiecki, and even more ashamed of himself. He could feel himself blushing, which almost never happened to him. Turning away from the lieutenant, he avoided questioning or even looking at any more wounded men, and found his way to the dressing station.

Forcing his way with difficulty up the steps, and through the walking wounded and the stretcher bearers bringing in more wounded men and coming out with dead ones, Galtsin entered the first room, took a quick look, and could not help turning straight back and running out into the street. It was all too frightful!

8

THE SPACIOUS, dark, high-ceilinged hall, lit only by the four or five candles carried by the doctors when they made their way to examine their patients, was absolutely full up. Stretcher bearers were constantly arriving with more wounded men, whom they set down side by side on the floor. The floor was already so crowded that the wretched men jostled up against one another, smearing each other with their blood. Meanwhile the stretcher parties left to bring in more wounded. The pools of blood that could be seen wherever there was an empty space, the fevered breathing of several hundred men, and the sweating of the stretcher bearers, combined to produce a characteristic thick, heavy, stinking miasma through which four candles glimmered faintly from different corners of the room. A murmur of groans, sighs and wheezes filled the room, interrupted now and then by a piercing scream. The nurses, whose calm faces were not filled with the usual vacant feminine expression of morbidly tearful compassion, but with practical, active concern, were picking their way over wounded men, flitting hither and thither among bloodstained greatcoats and shirts, bearing medicines, water, bandages and lint. Grim-faced doctors in rolled-up shirtsleeves knelt by their wounded patients, in the light of candles held up by a medical attendant, probing bullet wounds with their fingers, palpating the flesh around them, turning over severed limbs still attached to their bodies, and ignoring the dreadful groans and pleas of the sufferers. One of the doctors was sitting at a little table by the door; as Galtsin came in, he was just registering patient number 532.

'Ivan Bogaev, private, 3rd company, S—— regiment, compound fracture of femur,' another doctor shouted from the far end of the room, examining a soldier's shattered leg. 'Turn him over for me.'

'Oh, my fathers, please, fathers, don't!' the soldier cried out, begging them not to touch him.

'Perforated skull.'

'Semyon Neferdov, lieutenant-colonel, N—— infantry regiment. Stick it out, Colonel, or I can't do anything, I'll have to give up,' said a third doctor, poking some kind of hook into the head of the wretched lieutenant-colonel.

'Ay! Ay! Stop it! Oh, for the love of God, get it over with, get it over, for… A-a-a-ah!'

'Perforated chest… Sevastyan Sereda, private, what regiment? Oh, don't bother writing it down, he's dying. Take him away,' said the doctor, walking away from the soldier, whose eyes had rolled up as he breathed his death rattle.

Some forty stretcher bearers stood at the door, waiting to transport the wounded to hospital and the dead to the chapel. They observed the scene in silence; from time to time one of them would utter a deep sigh…

9

On his way to the bastion, Kalugin encountered a great many wounded men; but knowing from experience what a bad effect the sight of them would have on a man about to go into battle, he not only avoided stopping to ask questions—he tried to take no notice of them at all. At the foot of the hill he met an orderly racing down from the bastion at full gallop.

'Zobkin! Zobkin! Stop a minute!'

'What is it, sir?'

'Where have you come from?'

'The lodgements.'

'What's it like there? Hot, is it?'

'It's hell there. Terrible!'

And the orderly galloped off.

And indeed, although there was not much small-arms fire, the cannonade had started again, with new and ferocious intensity.

'Oh dear, that's bad!' thought Kalugin, with an unpleasant feeling inside him. He too was suffering a premonition, or rather a very commonplace thought—the thought of death. But Kalugin was no Staff Captain Mikhailov: he was proud, and possessed nerves of iron. In a word, he was what is called a brave man. He did not yield to his immediate reaction, but set about raising his spirits. He remembered a certain adjutant—one of Napoleon's, he thought—who, after delivering the orders entrusted to him, had galloped straight back to Napoleon at full tilt, his head covered in blood.

'*Vous êtes blessé?*' Napoleon had asked.

'*Je vous demande pardon, sire, je suis tué.*'* And the adjutant fell from his horse and died on the spot.

Kalugin found this an excellent story, and rather fancied himself as that adjutant. Then he lashed his horse on, assumed an even more daredevil Cossack posture, looked round at the Cossack following behind him at a fast trot, and galloped off in dashing style to the place where he was to dismount. Here he found four soldiers sitting on the stones smoking their pipes.

'What are you doing here?' he shouted at them.

'We'd just brought down a wounded man, your Honour, and sat down for a rest,' one of them replied, hiding his pipe behind his back and taking off his cap.

'Rest, indeed! Back to your posts, quick march! Or I'll report you to your regimental commander!'

And he joined them to go uphill along the trench, meeting wounded men at every step. When he reached the top, he took the trench leading off to the left, and after following it a little way, found himself completely alone. A shell splinter buzzed close by him and smacked into the trench wall. Another bomb flew up in the air right ahead of him and seemed to be making straight for him. Suddenly he felt afraid. He ran on four or five steps and fell to the ground. But when the bomb exploded, quite far away, he felt really annoyed with himself, and stood up to look round in case anyone had seen him fall. But there was no one.

Once fear has found its way into a man's soul, it is not quick to give way to any other emotion. Kalugin, who had always

* 'Are you wounded?' ...— 'Your pardon, sire, I am killed.'

boasted that he never ducked, now quickened his pace and hurried along the trench almost on all fours. 'Oh, this is no good!' he thought as he stumbled. 'They're sure to kill me.' Feeling his chest tightening and the sweat breaking out all over his body, he was surprised at himself, but no longer tried to overcome these feelings.

All at once he heard footsteps ahead. Quickly he straightened up, raised his head and walked on, rattling his sabre and moving not quite so fast as before. He hardly recognized himself. Soon he met a sapper officer and a sailor coming towards him. The officer shouted 'Get down!' pointing at the bright spot of a bomb which grew brighter and brighter as it approached, faster and faster, till it crunched into the earth near the trench. But Kalugin just slightly lowered his head, in an instinctive reaction to that shout of alarm, and carried on walking.

'That's a cool one!' said the sailor, who had watched the falling bomb with complete equanimity, his practised eye instantly telling him that none of its fragments could hit the trench. 'Didn't even bother to lie down.'

Kalugin was only a few steps away from crossing the open ground to reach the bastion commander's dugout when he felt everything going black again, and succumbed to the same idiotic terror; his heart started pounding, the blood rushed to his head, and he had to force himself to run on to reach the dugout.

'Why so breathless?' asked the general, when Kalugin had delivered the orders he had brought.

'Walking very fast, your Excellency!'

'Won't you have a glass of wine?'

Kalugin drank off a glass of wine and lit a cigarette. The engagement had already ended, though a heavy cannonade continued from both sides. The dugout was occupied by General N——, the bastion commander, and half a dozen other officers including Praskukhin, all discussing various details of the action. Sitting in this cosy room with its pale-blue hangings, a couch, a bed, a table with papers on it, a wall clock and an icon with a lamp burning before it, and looking at these signs of habitation and at the solid two-foot-thick beams which formed its ceiling, and listening to the gunfire which sounded so faint inside the dugout, Kalugin could not understand how he had twice given way to such inexcusable weakness. He was angry with himself, and longed for some danger so that he could put himself to the test once again.

'Ah, now, I'm glad you're here too, Captain,' he said to a naval officer in a staff officer's greatcoat, sporting a large moustache and a St George Cross. This officer had just entered the dugout to ask the general for some men to repair two embrasures on his battery, which had been buried in falling earth. 'My general ordered me to find out from you,' Kalugin went on, once the battery commander had finished his conversation with the general, 'whether your guns are capable of firing grapeshot into the enemy trenches.'

'I've only one gun that could do that,' answered the captain morosely.

'Still, let's go and have a look.'

The captain scowled and grunted crossly.

'I've just spent the whole night standing out there, and now I've come in to get a bit of rest,' he said. 'Couldn't you go on your own? My assistant, Lieutenant Karz, is out there—he can show you everything.'

This captain had spent the last six months in command of this battery, one of the most dangerous. Ever since the start of the siege, even before any dugouts had been built, he had lived on the bastion, and among the sailors he had the reputation of a brave man. So Kalugin found his refusal particularly surprising and shocking.

'So much for reputations!' he thought.

'Well then, I'll go alone, with your permission,' he told the captain with a touch of sarcasm; the captain, however, paid him no attention whatever.

But Kalugin had not considered that he had served, all in all, some fifty hours on the bastions, while the captain had lived there for six months. Kalugin was still at the stage of being driven by vanity—the desire to shine out, the hope of military honours and a fine reputation, the attraction of risk; while the captain had already been through all that. In the beginning he had enjoyed flattering his vanity, putting on a show of courage, taking unnecessary risks, in the hope of honours and a reputation—and had received them too; but now all these incentives had lost their hold over him, and he took a different view. He carried out his duties to the letter; but realizing very clearly now how slim his chances were of staying alive, after his six months on the bastion he no longer jeopardized those chances unless strictly necessary. So the young lieutenant, who had only arrived on the battery a week before and was now showing Kalugin over it (with both men pointlessly showing off, poking their heads out of the embrasures and climbing up onto the banquettes) looked ten times braver than the captain.

Having inspected the battery, Kalugin made his way back to the dugout; in the darkness he ran into the general, who was going to the watchtower with his orderlies.

'Captain Praskukhin,' the general was saying, 'would you step down to the right-hand lodgement and tell the second battalion of the M—— regiment, who are working there, to drop what they're doing, withdraw without making a sound, and rejoin their regiment which is standing at the foot of the hill in reserve. Got that? Take them down to the regiment yourself.'

'Yes, sir.'

And Praskukhin ran off to the lodgement.

The firing was slackening off.

10

'IS THIS THE SECOND battalion of the M—— regiment?' asked Praskukhin, reaching his destination and running up against some soldiers carrying sacks of earth.

'Yes, sir.'

'Where's your commander?'

Mikhailov, supposing that the company commander was wanted, climbed up out of his dugout, and taking Praskukhin for a senior officer, approached him with his hand to his cap.

'The general has ordered… you… you're to go… at once… and above all, as quietly as you can… to the rear, no, not the rear, but to join the reserves,' said Praskukhin, with a sidelong look at the enemy's fire.

Recognizing Praskukhin, Mikhailov dropped his hand, and once he had understood the order, he passed it on. The battalion bustled merrily into action, the soldiers gathered up their guns, put on their greatcoats and moved off.

No one who has not experienced it can imagine the profound relief a man feels when, having gone through a three hours' bombardment, he is allowed to leave such a dangerous position as the lodgements. During those three hours, Mikhailov had several times decided that his end had come, and several times covered with kisses all the icons he had with him; in the end he had grown somewhat calmer, convinced that he was certain to be killed and that he no longer belonged to this world. And yet it still cost him a great effort to control his legs and stop them running off when he, with Praskukhin at his side, led his company out of the lodgements.

'Goodbye,' said a major to him; he was the commander of another battalion which was staying in the lodgements, with whom Praskukhin had shared his soapy cheese, sitting in their dugout next to the parapet. 'Safe journey!'

'And you have a safe stay! Things seem to have quietened down now.'

But no sooner had he said this than the enemy, no doubt noticing the movement in the lodgements, fired off their cannon faster and faster. Our troops fired back, and once again an intense cannonade began. The stars gleamed faintly in the sky; the night was so dark, you could hardly see your hand in front of your face. Only the flashes of gunfire and the explosions of shells momentarily illuminated what lay around them. The soldiers hurried on in silence, involuntarily overtaking one another. All they could hear above the incessant booming of the cannon fire was the regular sound of their footsteps on the dry path, the clash of one bayonet against another, or some fearful soldier's sigh and prayer: 'O Lord, Lord, what was that?' Sometimes a wounded man's groan would be heard, and a cry of 'Stretcher here!' (The company under Mikhailov's command had lost twenty-six men from artillery fire alone that night.) A lightning flash on the distant, murky horizon, and the sentry on the bastion would call out 'Ca-a-annon!' and a cannonball would buzz over the company's head, throwing up earth and stones as it landed.

'Why the devil are they moving so slowly?' Praskukhin said to himself, constantly looking over his shoulder as he marched on beside Mikhailov. 'Honestly, I ought to run ahead—after all, I've passed on the order… But no, I'd better not, or this animal here might start telling people I was a coward, just as I did about him yesterday. Whatever happens, happens—I'll walk on beside him.'

'Why is he sticking to me like this?' Mikhailov was thinking meanwhile. 'Seems to me he always brings me bad luck. Here's another one making straight for us, I'm sure.'

Several hundred paces further on they ran into Kalugin, who was dashingly rattling his sabre as he made his way to the lodgements; the general had ordered him to find out how the earthworks were proceeding. But having met Mikhailov, it occurred to him that rather than going up there himself, under this fearful hail of gunfire—which he had not even been ordered to do—he could find out about it all in detail from an officer who had come from there. And indeed, Mikhailov gave him a detailed account of the works, though while doing so he afforded Kalugin no little amusement, for while Kalugin appeared to take no notice of the shooting at all, Mikhailov kept cowering down every time a shell exploded (sometimes very far away), ducking his head and constantly repeating with great conviction that 'that one's heading straight this way'.

'Look, Captain, here's one making straight for us,' said Kalugin to tease him, giving him a prod. After walking on a little further with them, Kalugin turned off into the trench leading to the general's dugout. 'You couldn't call him particularly brave, this captain,' he thought as he passed through the entrance.

'Well, what's the news?' asked the only officer in the room, who was sitting eating his supper.

'Oh, nothing; it seems to be more or less over.'

'What do you mean, over? Not at all—the general's just gone back out to the watchtower. Another regiment has arrived. There, do you hear it? More small-arms fire. Don't go out. Why should you?' the officer added, noticing Kalugin making a move to leave.

'I really ought to be out there, definitely I ought,' thought Kalugin. 'But I've taken plenty of risks today anyway. I hope I can serve for something better than cannon fodder.'

'Yes, you're right,' he said. 'I'd better wait for them here.'

And indeed, some twenty minutes later the general returned with his suite of officers. They included Baron Pest, but not Praskukhin. The Russian forces had beaten off the enemy and retaken the lodgements.

After hearing a detailed account of the action, Kalugin left the dugout, accompanied by Pest.

11

'YOUR GREATCOAT is all covered in blood: you weren't in the hand-to-hand fighting, were you?' Kalugin asked.

'Oh, my dear chap, it was terrible! Just imagine...'—and Pest began describing how he had been leading the whole company, how his company commander had been killed, how he had bayoneted a Frenchman, and how but for him all would have been lost, and so on and so forth.

The essential facts of his story—that the company commander had been killed and that Pest had killed a Frenchman—were true; but in describing the details, Cadet Pest was inventing things and boasting. He did not mean to boast, but could not help it, because throughout the action he had been overcome by a sort of fog of oblivion—everything that happened seemed to him to be happening somewhere else, to someone else and at some other time. Very naturally, he had been trying to resurrect all these details in a favourable light for himself. But the true facts were these.

The battalion to which he had been assigned for the sortie had spent a couple of hours under fire, sheltering behind a rampart. Then the battalion commander ahead of him gave an order, the company commanders moved off, and the battalion advanced beyond the rampart, halting a hundred paces further on and forming columns of one company each. Pest was told to position himself on the right flank of the second company.

With no idea where he was or why, he took up his post, involuntarily holding his breath and with cold shivers running down his spine as he peered dumbly into the black distance and waited for something terrible to happen. He was actually filled not so much with fear (since there was no firing) as with a feeling of weird strangeness at the fact of being here, outside the fortress, on open ground. Once again the battalion commander ahead of him said something. And again the officers whispered to one another, passing on the orders, and the black wall of the first company suddenly dropped out of sight. They had been ordered to lie down. The second company lay down too, and Pest, as he lowered himself, pricked his hand on something sharp. Only the commander of the second company did not lie down; his short figure remained upright, brandishing his sword as he moved about in front of his men, talking incessantly to them.

'Now then, men! We'll put up a fine show! Don't waste your bullets, go for the scum with your bayonets. When I call "Hurrah!", follow me close, don't fall back… Main thing is to keep close together… We'll show what we're made of, we won't fall flat on our faces, eh, boys? For our father, the Tsar!' he shouted, sprinkling his speech with oaths and waving his arms about in a terrifying way.

'What's our company commander called?' Pest asked the cadet lying by his side. 'Isn't he brave!'

'Yes, he's always like that in a fight,' replied the cadet. 'His name's Lisinkovsky.'

At that moment a sheet of flame shot up right in front of the company, there was a tremendous explosion, and stones and bomb fragments flew hissing high into the air. (At least fifty seconds later, one stone fell from the sky and smashed a soldier's foot.) This was a high-angle trajectory mortar bomb, and the fact that it had hit the company was proof that the French had observed the column.

'Mortar bombs, is it, then? The bastards… the filthy swine… Wait till we get to you, we'll give you a taste of our three-edged Russian bayonets, you sods!' the company commander shouted, so loud that the battalion commander had to order him to keep his voice down and make less noise.

Now the first company got to their feet, then the second; they were ordered to port arms, and the battalion advanced. Pest was so terrified, he had no recollection of how long it took, or where they were going, or who they were, or what they were doing. He walked on like a drunken man. But suddenly a million lights flashed out on every side, there was a whistling, and a crackling, and he yelled out and ran somewhere because everyone else was running and yelling. Then he tripped over and fell over something—it was his company commander, who had been wounded at the head of his company, and taking Cadet Pest for a Frenchman, seized him by the foot. He tore his foot free and raised himself up, but someone ran into him from behind and almost knocked him down again. Some other man yelled 'Run him through! What are you waiting for?' and someone took a musket and plunged the bayonet into something soft. '*À moi, camarades! Ah, sacré b… Ah! Dieu!*'* someone screamed in a terrifying, piercing voice, and only then did Pest realize that he had bayoneted a Frenchman.

A cold sweat broke out all over his body, he shook as though in a fever, and threw his musket on the ground. But that only lasted an instant; then it suddenly occurred to him that he was a hero. He picked up his musket, joined the other men shouting 'Hurrah!' and ran away from the dead Frenchman, while another soldier at once began pulling off the man's boots. Twenty paces further

* 'This way, boys! Oh, blasted… Oh, God!'

on, he reached a trench, where he found Russian soldiers and the battalion commander.

'I got one of them with my bayonet, sir!' he told the battalion commander.

'Well done, Baron!..'

12

'BUT YOU KNOW, Praskukhin's been killed,' said Pest, seeing off Kalugin who was going back to his quarters.

'No, really?'

'Definitely—I saw him myself.'

'Well, goodbye, I'm in a hurry.'

'I'm very pleased,' thought Kalugin as he reached his quarters. 'That's the first time I've had some good luck when I've been on duty. It was a great action—I'm alive and well, they'll be handing out splendid decorations, and I'm bound to get a golden sabre. And I deserve it, too.'

He reported all the necessary details to the general, and then returned to his room; here he found Prince Galtsin, who had been back for some time and was waiting for him, reading *Splendeurs et misères des courtisanes** which he had found on Kalugin's table.

Realizing that he was back home again and out of danger, Kalugin experienced an extraordinary sense of pleasure as he put on his nightshirt and lay down in bed. He told Galtsin all about the action, recounting it in the most natural way, from a viewpoint that proved what a thoroughly efficient and courageous officer

---

* *The Splendours and Miseries of Courtesans*, a novel by Balzac. One of those delightful books which have recently flooded the market, and which for some reason are particularly popular among our young people. [*Note by Tolstoy*]

he was. Though it appears to me personally that there was no need to point this out, since everyone knew it and no one had the slightest right or reason to doubt it—perhaps with the exception of the late Captain Praskukhin. Although Praskukhin had generally regarded it as an honour to walk arm in arm with Kalugin, he had only the day before confided to a friend of his that Kalugin was a very fine fellow, but 'strictly between ourselves', he had a terrible aversion to going out to the bastions.

This was what had happened. Praskukhin was walking beside Mikhailov, having just parted from Kalugin; and as they reached a slightly safer area, he was beginning to get his spirits back when he saw a lightning flash behind him and heard the sentry's shout of 'Mortar!' One of the soldiers following behind him said 'That one's coming straight for the battalion!'

Mikhailov looked round. The bright pinpoint of a bomb seemed to be hanging motionless at the top of its trajectory—the moment at which it is completely impossible to judge its direction. But that only lasted a second. Then the bomb began to fall, faster and faster, closer and closer, until one could see the sparks from its fuse and hear its ominous whistling as it made straight for the middle of the battalion.

'Get down!' came someone's frightened voice.

Mikhailov fell forward onto his stomach. Praskukhin instinctively bent double and screwed up his eyes; all he heard was the sound of the bomb thudding into the hard ground. A second went by, which felt like an hour, but the bomb did not explode. Praskukhin was frightened that his panic had been unnecessary—perhaps the bomb had fallen a long way away, and he was only imagining the fuse hissing right next to him. He opened his eyes, and saw with complacent satisfaction that Mikhailov, whom he still owed twelve and a half roubles, was lying on his stomach on the ground, motionless, pressing up against his feet and much lower than he was. But at that very moment his eyes rested on the glowing fuse of the mortar bomb, spinning on the ground a couple of feet away.

Horror seized hold of him, horror that shut out every other thought and sensation. He hid his face in his hands and fell to his knees.

Another second went by: a second during which a whole world of feelings, thoughts, hopes and memories flashed through his mind.

'Who's it going to kill, me or Mikhailov? Or both of us? If it's me, where'll it get me? If it's my head, then it's all over; but if it's my leg, they'll cut it off, and I'll tell them to make sure they use chloroform. And then I may survive. Or perhaps it'll only kill Mikhailov, and then I'll tell people about how we were walking side by side, and he was killed and I was covered with his blood. No, it's closer to me—I'll be the one.'

He remembered the twelve roubles he owed Mikhailov, and another debt he owed in Petersburg which he ought to have paid long ago; a Gipsy tune he had been humming that evening came back to him; the woman he loved came to his mind, in her bonnet with lilac ribbons; and a man who had insulted him five years ago, and whom he had never paid back... But along with these and thousands of other memories, he never lost for an instant his awareness of the present, and his expectation of horror and death. 'Well, perhaps it won't explode,' he thought, and with desperate determination he tried to open his eyes. But at that very instant, a red fire shone through his closed eyelids, and something shoved him in the middle of his chest with a fearful crunch. He set off running blindly, tripped over his sword which had slipped down under his feet, and fell on his side.

'Thank God! I'm only bruised,' was his first thought, and he tried to feel his chest with his hands. But his arms seemed to be bound fast, and his head felt as if it was held in a vice. Soldiers passed before his eyes, and unconsciously he counted them: 'One soldier, two, three, and the one in the turned-up greatcoat is an officer,' he thought; then lightning flashed before his eyes, and he wondered what sort of shot had been fired, a mortar or a cannon. Must have been a cannon; and there was another shot, and here were more soldiers—five, six, seven of them, all going past him. Suddenly he was frightened of being trampled, and wanted to cry out that he was bruised; but his mouth was so dry that his tongue stuck to the roof of it, and he felt desperately thirsty. He could feel the wetness around his chest, and the sense of wetness made him think of water. He even felt like drinking whatever was wet there. 'I must be bleeding from that fall,' he thought, and became more and more frightened that the soldiers who kept flashing past him would crush him. Summoning all his strength, he tried to shout 'Take me with you!'—but instead of that he uttered such a dreadful groan that the very sound of it scared him. Then red lights began to flash before his eyes, and he had the feeling that the soldiers were piling stones on top of him. The flashing lights began to fade, and the stones piled on top of him pressed heavier and heavier on him. He made an effort to shove the stones away, and stretched out his body; but after that he no longer saw, nor heard, nor thought, nor felt anything more. He had been killed outright by a bomb splinter in the middle of his chest.

13

WHEN MIKHAILOV saw the bomb coming, he fell to the ground, screwed up his eyes and opened and shut them twice just like Praskukhin, and just like him went through an endless succession of thoughts and emotions during the two seconds that the bomb lay on the ground before it exploded. In his thoughts he prayed to God and repeated over and over again 'Thy will be done!' But at the same time he thought: 'Why on earth did I volunteer to join the army? And even got transferred to the infantry so as to join in this campaign? Wouldn't it have been better to stay in T—— with the Uhlans, and spend time with my dear Natasha… instead of which, look where I am now!' And he began counting: one, two, three, four, telling himself that if it blew up on an even number he would survive, but if it was an odd number he'd be killed. 'That's it! I'm killed!' he thought when the bomb exploded (he didn't remember whether it was on an even or odd number), and he felt a blow on his head and an agonizing pain. 'Oh Lord, forgive me my sins!' he said, flinging up his hands. He tried to raise himself, and fell back unconscious.

The first thing he was aware of when he came round was blood trickling down his nose, and the pain in his head which was much less severe now. 'That's my soul leaving my body,' he thought. 'What'll it be like there? Lord, receive my soul in peace. But it's an odd thing—even though I'm dying, I can hear the soldiers' voices so clearly, and the sound of gunfire.'

'Stretcher here! Hey! Company commander's killed!' a voice called out above his head. He realized he knew that voice—it was drummer Ignatyev.

Someone took hold of him by the shoulders. He managed to open his eyes, and saw the deep-blue sky overhead, groups of stars, and two bombs flying over, one gaining on the other. He saw Ignatyev, the soldiers carrying guns and a stretcher, the earth bank of the trench, and suddenly he could believe that he was not yet in the next world.

He had received a slight head wound from a stone. His first reaction was almost one of regret: he had prepared himself so well and so peacefully to pass over to the other side that it felt disagreeable to return to reality with its bombs, trenches, soldiers and blood. His next reaction was a sense of unthinking joy at being alive; and after that—fear, and a longing to get away from the bastion as quickly as he could. The drummer bandaged up his commander's head with a handkerchief, took him by the arm and led him off towards the dressing station.

'Just a minute—where am I going, and what for?' the staff captain wondered when he had collected his thoughts a little. 'My duty is to stay with my company,' a little voice whispered to him, 'not go on ahead, particularly as the company will soon be out of firing range too. And if I stay at my post after being wounded—I'm bound to get a decoration.'

'No, there's no need for this, lad,' he said, pulling his arm free from the obliging drummer, who himself was mainly anxious to get away as quickly as he could. 'I shan't go to the dressing station—I'm staying with my company.'

And he turned back.

'You really ought to get that properly bandaged, your Honour,' said Ignatyev timidly. 'It only seems like nothing to you, because you're in the heat of a battle; but it'll get worse if you don't get it seen to. And look how things are heating up back there… honestly, your Honour.'

Mikhailov paused irresolutely for a minute, and probably would have followed Ignatyev's advice, if he had not remembered an episode he had witnessed at the dressing station some days back. An officer with a slight scratch on his hand had come in to have it dressed, and when the doctors saw him, they smiled; one of them—a man with side whiskers—had even told him that he'd never die from a wound like that, and one could do oneself more damage with a table fork.

'Maybe they'll be just as unimpressed with my wound, and smile at it—and even say something like that,' thought the staff captain, and turned resolutely back to rejoin his company, ignoring the drummer's arguments.

'Where's that orderly officer Praskukhin who was with me?' he asked the ensign who was leading his company when he reached him.

'I don't know—I believe he was killed,' the ensign answered reluctantly. He was very annoyed that the staff captain had reappeared, thus depriving him of the pleasure of claiming to have been the only officer left in the company.

'Killed—or wounded? How can you not know, when he was walking along with us? And why didn't you bring him along?'

'How could anyone bring a man along in the middle of this firestorm?'

'Really, Mikhail Ivanovich,' said Mikhailov angrily, 'how could you abandon him, if he was alive? And even if he was killed, you still ought to have picked up his body! Say what you like, but he was the general's orderly officer, and he might still be alive.'

'How can he be alive? I'm telling you, I went up myself and saw him,' protested the ensign. 'For goodness' sake! It's all we can do to get our own men out of here. Look at them, the bastards! Sending cannonballs at us, now!' he added, ducking. Mikhailov ducked too, grabbing hold of his head which hurt terribly from the sudden movement.

'No, we absolutely have to go and pick him up. He might still be alive,' said Mikhailov. 'It's our duty, Mikhail Ivanich!'

Mikhail Ivanich said nothing.

'If he'd been a good officer, he'd have picked him up right then—but now we have to send off some soldiers on their own. And how can we send them? Under this dreadful fire, they might get killed for nothing,' thought Mikhailov.

'Listen, men! We've got to go back to pick up an officer who's lying wounded up there in the ditch,' he said, not too loudly or peremptorily, feeling how reluctant the soldiers would be to carry out his order. And naturally, since he was not addressing anyone in particular, nobody stepped forward to do so.

'Sergeant! Over here!'

The sergeant apparently did not hear him, and carried on marching forward with the rest.

'Well, perhaps it's true that he's already dead, and it's *not worth* putting men in unnecessary danger—it's all my fault for not seeing to it before. I'll go back myself to check if he's alive. That's my *duty*,' Mikhailov told himself.

'Mikhail Ivanich! Lead the company on, I'll catch up with you,' he said, and picking up the skirts of his greatcoat with one hand while with the other repeatedly touching the little icon of St Metrophanes (a saint in whom he had particular faith), he ran back along the trench, almost on his hands and knees, and trembling with terror.

Once he had assured himself that his fellow officer was dead, Mikhailov dragged himself back, still panting, ducking and holding the loosened bandage in place on his head, which had started aching badly. The battalion was now in its place at the foot of the hill, almost out of the enemy's range, when Mikhailov reached it. Almost out of range, I repeat; but even here, stray bombs still fell from time to time, and that night one captain was killed by a bomb fragment as he sat out the battle in one of the sailors' dugouts.

'Still, I'd best go to the dressing station tomorrow to get myself registered,' thought the staff captain, while having his head wound dressed by a newly arrived medical orderly. 'That'll help towards a decoration.'

14

HUNDREDS OF FRESH, bloodstained corpses of men who only two hours ago had been filled with all kinds of hopes and longings, lofty and trivial, now lay with stiffened limbs on the grass of the dew-covered, flowering valley that stretched between the bastion and the trench, or on the smooth floor of the Chapel of the Dead in Sevastopol. Hundreds of men, with curses and prayers on their parched lips, crawled, writhed and groaned, some among the corpses in the flowering valley, others on stretchers, camp beds, or the bloodstained floor of the dressing station; and yet, just as on previous days, the summer lightning once more flickered over Mount Sapun, the glimmering stars faded, a white mist drifted in off the dark, grumbling sea, the crimson light of dawn flared up in the east, the long purple cloudlets spread over the pale azure horizon, and just as on previous days, promising joy, love and happiness to all the awakening world, the sun's mighty and magnificent orb rose out of the sea.

15

THE NEXT EVENING the military band was again playing on the boulevard, and again officers, cadets, soldiers and young women were strolling festively around the pavilion and along the lower avenues of fragrant flowering white acacias.

Kalugin, Prince Galtsin and a colonel were walking arm in arm by the pavilion, talking about yesterday's engagement. The main theme of their conversation, as always in such situations, was not the action itself, but the part each of them had played in it, and the courage he had shown. Their expressions and voices were all serious, almost mournful, as though each of them was closely affected and grieved by the day's losses; but if the truth be told, none of them had lost anyone particularly close to him (indeed, are people ever particularly close in army life?), so this air of grief was no more than an official attitude which they felt they had to voice. In fact both Kalugin and the colonel would have been happy to see an engagement of this sort every day, so long as they were awarded a golden sword every time and the rank of major-general; though they were all of them splendid fellows. I like the way some conqueror may find himself described as a monster for having destroyed millions of people in the name of his own ambition; but just find out the honest views of Ensign Petrushov, Second Lieutenant Antonov and the rest of them, each a little Napoleon, a little monster happy to start a battle and kill off a hundred men or so, for no more than an extra star or a rise of one third in his pay.

'No, I'm sorry,' said the colonel, 'it all started off on the left flank. I was there, after all.'

'That may be so,' answered Kalugin; 'I spent more time over on the right flank. Went there twice, once to find the general, and the second time just to see how things were going by the lodgements. That's where things really got hot.'

'Yes, I'm sure Kalugin knows how it went,' Prince Galtsin said to the colonel. 'You know, V—— was telling me just today that you put up a splendid show.'

'But the losses—the losses were terrible,' said the colonel in a tone of official sorrow. 'Four hundred men from my own regiment. It's astonishing that I got out alive.'

At that moment the lilac-coated figure of Mikhailov, with his worn-down boots and bandaged head, appeared at the far end of the boulevard, making his way towards these gentlemen. He was greatly embarrassed at the sight of them, remembering how he had ducked in Kalugin's presence, and it occurred to him that they might think he was only pretending to be wounded. If the gentlemen had not been looking his way, he would have run down the boulevard and gone home, resolving not to come out again till he could take off his bandage.

'*Il fallait voir dans quel état je l'ai rencontré hier sous le feu*,'* said Kalugin with a smile as they were coming towards each other.

'What's this—are you wounded, Captain?' Kalugin asked him, with a smile that signified 'Well, did you see me yesterday? Pretty good, wasn't I?'

'Yes, a bit—by a stone,' answered Mikhailov, blushing, with a

* 'You should have seen the state he was in when I came across him under fire yesterday.'

face that said 'Yes, I saw you, and I admit you were splendid, but I'm a terrible, terrible coward.'

'*Est-ce que le pavillon est baissé déjà?*'* asked Prince Galtsin, again with that haughty expression of his, staring at the staff captain's cap and addressing no one in particular.

'*Non, pas encore*,'† replied Mikhailov, anxious to show that he too knew how to speak French.

'Is the truce really still on?' asked Galtsin, politely addressing him in Russian and thereby conveying—so it seemed to the staff captain—that 'you'll no doubt find it difficult speaking French, so why not simply…?' And on that note the adjutants walked on.

Just as on the day before, the staff captain felt utterly alone. So after exchanging bows with various gentlemen, some of whom he preferred not to talk to, and others whom he did not dare approach—he sat down beside the Kazarsky Monument and lit a cigarette.

Baron Pest had also come out onto the boulevard. He was telling a story about how he had been present when the truce was signed, and had talked with some French officers, and claimed that one of them had said to him: '*S'il n'avait pas fait clair encore pendant une demi-heure, les embuscades auraient été reprises*,' and how he had replied: '*Monsieur! Je ne dis pas non, pour ne pas vous donner un démenti*,'‡ and what a good riposte that had been, and so forth.

In point of fact, although he had been present when the truce was signed, he had never managed to say anything particularly witty there, though he had been terribly keen to talk with the French officers (after all, it was such fun talking to Frenchmen).

---

* 'Has the flag been lowered yet?'

† 'No, not yet.'

‡ 'If it had stayed dark for another half-hour, the lodgements would have been retaken,' …— 'Sir! I don't deny it, merely so as not to contradict you.'

Cadet Baron Pest had spent a long time walking up and down the lines, asking any Frenchman nearby: '*De quel régiment êtes-vous?*'* The French soldiers had answered him, and that was it. But when he ventured too far behind the lines, the French sentry, unaware that this soldier knew French, swore at him in the third person. '*Il vient regarder nos travaux, ce sacré c...*,'† he said, and in consequence Baron Pest, finding nothing of any further interest in the truce, set off back to his quarters, thinking up on his way all those French phrases he was now boasting about.

Captain Zobov was also out on the boulevard, talking at the top of his voice, and Captain Obzhogov looking dishevelled, and the artillery captain who never curried favour with anyone, and the cadet who was so happy in love, and all the other characters of the day before, all still driven on by the same impulses of lying, vanity or just silliness. The only ones missing were Praskukhin, Neferdov and one or two others, whom practically no one there even remembered or thought about, although their bodies had not yet been washed, laid out and buried in the ground, and whose fathers, mothers, wives and children, if they had any, would also have forgotten them before the month was out, if they had not already done so.

'I almost didn't recognize this old guy here,' says a soldier who is clearing away the dead bodies, lifting by its shoulders a corpse with a stove-in chest, an enormous swollen head, a shiny blackened face and rolled-up eyes. 'Hold him up by the chest, Morozka, or he'll fall to bits. Ugh, what a stink!'

'Ugh, what a stink!'—that's all that was left of this man, for those who were still alive.

---

* 'Which regiment are you from?'

† 'He's come to look at our works, the damned b...'

16

WHITE FLAGS have been raised on our bastion and on the trench on the French side; and scattered here and there in the flowering valley between the two are little groups of mutilated corpses in grey or blue uniforms, all stripped of their boots. Working parties are lifting them up and loading them onto carts. The air is heavy with the horrible sickly stench of dead bodies. Crowds of people have ventured out of Sevastopol and the French camp to gaze at the spectacle, rushing to assemble together in eager, benevolent curiosity.

Listen to what these people are saying to one another. Here is a young officer surrounded by a group of Russians and French; his French is bad, but good enough to make himself understood. He is examining a French guardsman's pouch.

'*Et ceci pourquoi ce oiseau ici?*' he asks.

'*Parce que c'est une giberne d'un régiment de la garde, monsieur, qui porte l'aigle impérial.*'

'*Est vous de la garde?*'

'*Pardon, monsieur, du 6ième de ligne.*'

'*Et ceci où acheté?*'* asks the officer, pointing to a yellow wooden cigarette-holder in which the Frenchman is smoking a cigarette.

---

* 'And this, why this bird here?' …— 'Because it's the pouch of a Guards regiment, sir, and they carry the imperial eagle.' — 'Are you in the Guards?' — 'No, sir, the sixth regiment of the line.' — 'And this, where you bought?' [*The French spoken by this Russian officer is rather ungrammatical.*]

'*À Balaclave, monsieur! C'est tout simple—en bois de palme.*'[*]

'*Joli,*'[†] says the officer, guided through this conversation not so much by his own ideas as by the French words he knows.

'*Si vous voulez bien garder cela comme souvenir de cette rencontre, vous m'obligerez.*'[‡] And the courteous Frenchman extinguishes his cigarette and offers the officer his holder, with a little bow. The officer gives him his own in exchange, and everyone in the group, French as well as Russian, smiles and looks very pleased.

Here is a jaunty infantryman in a pink shirt, his greatcoat hanging over his shoulders, standing with a group of other soldiers, all with cheerful, inquisitive faces, hands behind their backs. He goes up to a Frenchman and asks for a light for his pipe. The Frenchman sucks at his own pipe to bring up a flame, and tips some of the burning tobacco into the Russian's pipe.

'*Tabac boon,*' says the soldier in the pink shirt, and his audience smiles.

'*Oui, bon tabac, tabac turc,*' says the Frenchman. '*Et chez vous tabac russe? Bon?*'[§]

'Roos boon' says the soldier in the pink shirt, while his audience rolls about with laughter. 'Fronsay no boon, bonjewer, monsiewer,' the soldier goes on, firing off his entire reserve of French words in a single volley, while patting the Frenchman on the stomach and laughing. The French soldiers laugh too.

'*Ils ne sont pas jolis, ces bêtes de russes,*'[¶] says a Zouave in the French group.

---

* 'At Balaclava, sir! It's very ordinary, made of palm wood.'

† 'Pretty.'

‡ 'If you would care to keep it as a keepsake of our meeting, I should be obliged to you.'

§ 'Yes, good tobacco, Turkish tobacco,' … 'And in your country, Russian tobacco? Good?'

¶ 'They're ugly creatures, these Russian brutes'

'*De quoi de ce qu'ils rient donc?*'* says another dark-skinned man with an Italian accent, coming over to the Russians.

'Caftan boon' says the jaunty soldier, examining the embroidered skirts of the Zouave's uniform, and everyone laughs again.

'*Ne sortez pas de la ligne, à vos places, sacré nom!*'† cries a French corporal. And with evident annoyance, the soldiers disperse.

And here is a ring of French officers surrounding a young Russian cavalry officer who is fairly showering them with French barber's argot. The talk is about a certain '*comte Sazonoff, que j'ai beaucoup connu, monsieur,*' in the words of a French officer with a single epaulette. '*C'est un de ces vrais comtes russes, comme nous les aimons.*'

'*Il y a un Sazonoff que j'ai connu,*' says the cavalry officer, '*mais il n'est pas comte, à moins que je sache, un petit brun de votre âge à peu près.*'

'*C'est ça, monsieur, c'est lui. Oh, que je voudrais le voir, ce cher comte. Si vous le voyez, je vous prie bien de lui faire mes compliments. Capitaine Latour,*'‡ he says, and bows.

'*N'est-ce pas terrible, la triste besogne que nous faisons? Ça chauffait cette nuit, n'est-ce pas?*'§ says the cavalry officer, trying to keep the conversation going and gesturing at the corpses.

---

* 'What are they laughing at?'

† 'Don't break ranks, back to your places, damn you!..'

‡ 'Oh yes, that's him, sir. Oh, how I'd love to see him, the dear count. If you see him, would you please give him my regards. I'm Captain Latour.'

§ '... Count Sazonoff, whom I knew very well, sir,' ...— 'One of those real Russian counts, the ones we like.'

'There's a Sazonoff whom I knew,' ... 'but he's not a count, as far as I know. A shortish man with brown hair, about your age.'

'Oh yes, that's him, sir. Oh, how I'd love to see him, the dear count. If you see him, would you please give him my regards. I'm Captain Latour.'...

'Isn't it terrible, this sad business we're in? It got lively last night, didn't it?'

'*Oh, monsieur, c'est affreux! Mais quels gaillards vos soldats, quels gaillards! C'est un plaisir que de se battre contre des gaillards comme eux.*'

'*Il faut avouer que les vôtres ne se mouchent pas du pied non plus,*'* says the cavalry officer, bowing and imagining that he is being extremely complimentary. But enough of this.

Look instead at this ten-year-old boy, wearing an old cap that had probably once been his father's, boots on his bare feet and a pair of nankeen breeches held up by a single suspender. He had come out from behind the ramparts as soon as the truce began, to wander up and down the hollow, staring with dumb curiosity at the French soldiers and the corpses lying on the ground, and picking the blue meadow flowers that studded this grim valley. Returning homewards with a big bunch of flowers and holding his nose against the smell which the wind carried towards him, he stopped by one of the piles of bodies already collected, and spent a long time staring at the one nearest to him, a dreadful headless corpse. After a long while he moved closer to touch its rigid outstretched arm with the tip of his foot. The arm twitched a little. He gave it a second prod with his foot, harder this time. The arm gave another twitch, and fell back into place again. Suddenly the boy screamed, buried his face in his flowers and rushed back to the fortress as fast as his legs would carry him.

Yes, the white flags are out on the bastion and along the trench, the flowering valley is filled with stinking corpses, the splendid sun sinks down towards the dark-blue sea, and the blue sea's swell glitters in the sun's golden beams. Thousands of people have come together, to look, talk and smile at one another. And

---

* 'Oh, it's dreadful, sir! But what fine lads your men are—such fine lads! It's a pleasure doing battle with fine lads like them.'

'I have to admit that your men also know their way about.'

these people, Christians who all confess the same great law of love and self-denial—when they look at what they have done, will they not instantly fall to their knees in repentance before Him who, when he gave them life, planted in each one's soul not only the fear of death, but the love of all that is good and beautiful? Will they not embrace one another as brothers, weeping tears of joy and happiness? No! Those bits of white cloth will be put away, and once more the weapons of death and suffering will whistle and thunder, innocent blood will be poured forth, and groans and curses fill the air.

There—I have said all I wanted to say, for now. But my heart is filled with a painful reflection. Perhaps I ought not to have said it. Perhaps what I have said belongs to one of those grim truths which lurk unperceived in each person's soul, but must not be spoken out loud for fear of doing harm—like the dregs of wine which must not be shaken up if the wine is not to be spoilt.

Where in this story is a depiction of evil to be avoided? Where is a depiction of good to be emulated? Who is the villain, and who the hero here? All are good and all are evil.

Neither Kalugin with his conspicuous show of gallantry (his *bravoure de gentilhomme*) and the vanity that informs all his actions, nor Praskukhin, a shallow, harmless fellow, for all that he fell in battle for faith, crown and country, nor Mikhailov with his timidity and blinkered outlook, nor Pest, a child with no firm convictions or principles—none of them can be either the heroes or the villains of my story.

The hero of my story, whom I love with all my heart and soul, whom I have tried to portray in all his beauty, and who has always been, is and will always remain magnificent—is the truth.

26 June 1855

SEVASTOPOL IN AUGUST 1855

1

AT THE END OF AUGUST, an officer's waggon (that strange form of transport, no longer seen anywhere these days, which was something between a Jew's *britzka*, a Russian cart and a wicker basket) was moving at a walking pace through the thick, hot dust of the main Sevastopol highway between Duvankoy* and Bakhchisaray, where the road runs through several gorges.

Squatting on his haunches in front, tugging on the reins, was the officer's servant wearing a nankeen frock coat and an officer's cap worn limp with age. In the back, on a heap of packages and bundles covered by a horse cloth, sat an infantry officer in his summer greatcoat. As far as one could tell from his seated position, this officer was not particularly tall, but had an exceptionally broad frame—not so much from shoulder to shoulder as from chest to back. Broad-bodied and thickset, he had taut, well-developed neck muscles front and back. He did not have what is known as a waist—a narrowing halfway along the trunk—but neither did he have a paunch; in fact he was rather on the thin side, especially his face, which was marked by an unhealthy yellowish tan. His face might have been handsome but for a certain puffiness and soft, deep wrinkles—not of old age—which exaggerated his features and made them run together, giving his whole face a coarse, stale

* The last post-house before Sevastopol. [*Note by Tolstoy*]

appearance. His smallish eyes were hazel-coloured and exceptionally lively, indeed mischievous; he had a thick moustache, not very wide, and rather chewed at the ends. His chin and particularly his cheekbones were covered with a two-day growth of very thick, black, bristly stubble. This officer had received a head wound from a bomb splinter on 10 May, and still wore a bandage on it; but for the past week he had been feeling completely recovered, and was now travelling from the Simferopol hospital to rejoin his regiment, which was stationed somewhere out there, where the noise of shots could be heard—but whether it was in Sevastopol, on the North Side, or at Inkerman, he had not so far been able to discover. The shooting could already be very clearly heard where he was, particularly when the wind was in the right quarter and there were no mountains in the way; it sounded quite intense and apparently quite close. Sometimes an explosion shook the air, making one flinch involuntarily; sometimes there would be a run of quieter sounds close together, like a drum roll, occasionally punctuated by a startling boom; sometimes it all merged into a kind of rolling crackle, like the peals of thunder one hears when a storm is at its height and the rain has just started pouring down. Everyone said that a terrible bombardment was under way, and one could clearly hear it going on. The officer was hurrying his servant along, clearly anxious to join his regiment as quickly as he could. Coming to meet them was a long train of Russian peasants who had taken provisions into Sevastopol and were now returning with sick and wounded soldiers in grey greatcoats, sailors in black overcoats, Greek volunteers in red fez caps and bearded militiamen. The officer's cart had to wait, and the officer himself, screwing up his face and eyes against the thick dust which hung in a motionless cloud over the road, penetrating his eyes and ears and sticking to his perspiring face, stared with resentful apathy at the faces of the sick and wounded men as they rolled past.

'Look, sir, that feeble little soldier's from our company,' said the servant to his officer, pointing to a cart filled with wounded men which had just drawn level with them.

Sitting sideways in the front of the cart was a bearded Russian peasant in a lambswool felt cap, busy tying the lash onto his whip while pressing the stock to his body with his elbow. Behind him in the cart, jolting this way and that, were five soldiers in a variety of postures. One of them, with his arm in a sling roughly held in place by a cord, and wearing a greatcoat draped across his shoulders over a very dirty shirt, though pale and thin, was sitting smartly upright in the middle of the cart, and made to take off his cap at the sight of this officer; but then, no doubt remembering that he was wounded, tried to pretend that he had only been going to scratch his head. Another man lay beside him on the very floor of the cart; all one could see of him was the two emaciated arms he had stretched out to hold on to the sides of the cart, and his raised knees flopping from side to side like bits of wet bast. A third man, with a swollen face, a bandage on his head, and a soldier's cap perched on top of it, was sitting sideways, dangling his legs down over the wheel; with his elbows propped on his knees, he seemed to be dozing. This was the man whom the officer addressed.

'Dolzhnikov!' he called out.

'Mm… present!' replied the soldier, opening his eyes and taking off his cap, in such a resonant, staccato bass voice that it sounded as if twenty soldiers were calling out in unison.

'When were you wounded, my man?'

The soldier's puffy, leaden-hued eyes lightened up. He had evidently recognized his officer.

'Your health, sir!' he called back in the same crisp bass voice.

'Where's the regiment stationed at present?'

'They were in Sevastopol, but they were going to be transferred on Wednesday, your Honour.'

'Where to?'

'Don't know... Probably the North Side, your Honour! Just today, your Honour,' he added in a drawn-out voice, putting on his cap again, 'he's started firing all over us, mostly bombs—they're even getting as far as the bay. Hammering us so hard today, it's just frightful...'

Nothing more could be made out, but his posture and the look on his face made it clear that he was full of the resentment of a man in pain, and uttering words of little comfort.

The officer in the cart, Lieutenant Kozeltsov, was not your average officer. He was not one of those men who live and act the way they do, and avoid doing other things, because that is how other people live their lives. He did whatever he pleased, and other people then followed his example and felt sure that this must be right. He was quite richly endowed by nature, being nobody's fool, and talented in many ways—a good singer who could play the guitar, had a way with words and wrote well. He was particularly good at official documents, having become a practised hand as the regimental adjutant. But his most remarkable quality was his unrelenting self-esteem, which, although largely fed by his many minor gifts, was itself a forceful and striking trait of his personality. His vanity had penetrated his whole life to such an extent, in a way most often seen in exclusively male and particularly military environments, that he could never see any choice before him but to outdo everyone else, or die. Even his inner impulses were driven by vanity; he liked to do better than anyone to whom he compared himself, just for his own satisfaction.

'Catch me listening to Moscow* going on at me!' he grumbled. His heart was filled with a sort of glum apathy, and his mind with a fog of confused thoughts brought on by the sight of the train of wounded men and the soldier's words, whose message was now being brought out and confirmed by the sounds of bombardment. 'Absurd, that Moscow... Get on with it, Nikolaev, press on... Hey, are you asleep?' he growled rather peevishly at his servant, adjusting the skirts of his greatcoat.

The reins gave a jerk, Nikolaev clicked his tongue, and the cart rolled on at a trot.

'We'll just pull up for a minute to feed the horses, and carry straight on, this very day,' said the officer.

* 'Moscow' or 'the oath' are half-contemptuous, half-affectionate terms used by the officers of many army regiments to refer to the common soldiers. [*Note by Tolstoy*]

2

AS SOON AS HE drove into the street lined by the ruins of Duvankoy's stone-walled Tatar houses, Lieutenant Kozeltsov was again held up by a military transport carrying mortar bombs and cannonballs to Sevastopol, whose carts were filling the whole road.

Two infantrymen were sitting on the stones of a ruined wall by the roadside, in the midst of all the dust, eating bread and watermelon.

'Going far, countryman?' one of them asked, munching his bread. He was addressing a soldier carrying a small shoulder bag who had stopped nearby.

'On my way to join my company; I've been away in the province,' replied the soldier, averting his eyes from the watermelon and adjusting the bag on his back. 'We've been away gathering hay for our company for three weeks or so, but suddenly they called us all back, see—only no one knows where our regiment is right now. Someone said our lot had been moved to the Korabelnaya last week. You haven't heard, have you, gents?'

'It's in the town, lad, in the town,' said the other man, an old convoy soldier, digging his clasp knife eagerly into the unripe whitish flesh of the watermelon. 'We only just left there this afternoon. It's godawful back there, lad, you'd best stay away—why not lie low in the hay somewhere for a day or two, you'll be a lot better off!'

'Why, how's that, gents?'

'Can't you hear? He's blazing away wherever you look, there's not a stone left standing. And what a lot of our boys he's killed—more than you could count!' The man made an eloquent gesture with his arm, and adjusted his cap.

The travelling soldier shook his head thoughtfully, tut-tutted a bit, then pulled his pipe out of his boot top, poked the half-burnt tobacco about without refilling it, lit a pinch of tinder from the soldier who was smoking, and raised his cap.

'Nobody but God, gentlemen! I bid you farewell!' he said, shook his pack into place on his back, and went on his way.

'Hey, you ought to wait a bit!' said the soldier who was digging out the melon, in a drawn-out, coaxing voice.

'All the same,' muttered the traveller, threading his way between the wheels of the carts that thronged the road, 'I suppose I ought to get myself a watermelon for supper, too, the way folks are talking.'

3

WHEN KOZELTSOV drove up to the post-house, it was full of people. The first person he met in the doorway, before even going in, was a thin, very young man, the postmaster. He was exchanging abuse with two officers, who had followed him out of the door.

'And it isn't three days you'll be waiting, more like ten! Even generals have to wait, my friend!' the postmaster said, happy to be spreading dismay. 'I'm not getting between the shafts myself, just to please you!'

'If there aren't any horses, you shouldn't be handing them out! How come there was a horse for that footman with all his baggage?' shouted the senior of the two officers, holding a glass of tea in his hands. He was so incensed, he could barely resist using offensively familiar language to the postmaster, and let the man feel it.

'You have to understand, Mr Postmaster,' began the younger officer, in a hesitant voice, 'we're not travelling for our own pleasure. I mean, they must be needing us there, mustn't they, if they've sent for us. This way, honestly, I'll have to let General Kramper know about you, definitely I will. I mean, the way you're behaving... you've got no respect for an officer's rank.'

'You always mess things up!' the older officer interrupted angrily. 'You always get in my way. You have to know how to talk to these people. Now he's lost all respect for us. Hey, you—horses here, this minute!'

'I'd be delighted, sir, but where am I to get them?'

The postmaster was silent for a moment. Then he suddenly became very agitated, making wild gestures with his arms, and said:

'Look here, sir, I understand what you're saying, I know all about it—but what am I supposed to do? Now just give me...' (at these words, hope dawned on the officers' faces) '... give me to the end of the month here without getting killed—and I'll have got out of this. I'd sooner be up on the Malakhov Heights than stay here. Honest to God! That lot can do whatever they like, if they run things like this. There's not a single decent cart left in the whole place, and the horses haven't seen a wisp of hay for three days.'

The postmaster disappeared out of the gate, while Kozeltsov and the two officers went indoors.

'Well, there you are,' the older officer said to the younger one in a perfectly calm voice, though a second earlier he had seemed to be in a fury. 'We've been on the road three months, we can wait a bit longer. Doesn't matter, we'll be in plenty of time.'

The dirty, smoke-filled room was so full of officers and their trunks that Kozeltsov could only find room to sit down by the window. Here he studied the faces around him and listened to their conversations, while rolling himself a cigarette. The main group of officers was sitting to the right of the door, by a crooked, greasy table on which stood two samovars with their brass turning green in places, and lumps of sugar in a variety of paper packets. Here a young clean-shaven officer in a new quilted kaftan, probably made out of a woman's dressing gown, was pouring water into a teapot. There were another four officers, no older than him, in various corners of the room. One of them was asleep on a divan, with a fur coat rolled up under his head; another was standing by a table carving a piece of roast mutton for an officer missing an arm, who was sitting by the table. Two other officers, one in an adjutant's greatcoat, the other in a thin infantry coat and with a cartridge pouch strapped across his shoulder, were sitting by the stove ledge; the very way in which they stared at the rest of the company, and the way the one with the cartridge pouch was smoking his cigar, made it quite clear that they were not front-line officers and were very pleased not to be. Not that they were in any way overtly contemptuous, but there was a sort of complacent serenity in their manner, founded partly on money, partly on their being in close relations with the generals—an awareness of their superiority, even extending to a wish to hide it. Then there was a young doctor with thick lips, and an artillery officer with a German-looking face, who were both sitting almost on the feet of the young officer asleep on the couch, and counting their money. And there were some four officers' servants, either dozing or attending to the trunks and bundles by the door.

Among all these people, Kozeltsov could not see a single one whom he recognized; but he listened to their conversations with some curiosity. He liked the look of the young officers, who, as he had concluded at first glance, had only just left the cadet corps—particularly as the sight of them reminded him that his brother, also an ex-cadet, was due to join one of the Sevastopol batteries in the next few days. But everything about the officer with the cartridge pouch, whose face seemed somehow familiar, struck him as insolent and repugnant. He even left his seat by the window to sit down on the stove ledge, thinking to himself: 'If he says anything, I'll put him in his place right away.' As a true front-line officer and a fine soldier, Kozeltsov not only disliked but resented staff officers, and a single look had confirmed to him that that was what those two men were.

4

'BUT IT'S AWFULLY ANNOYING,' one of the young officers was saying. 'Here we are, so close, and yet we simply can't get there. There might be some action today, and we won't be there.'

His squeaky voice and the pink patches that suddenly appeared on his youthful face were signs of the appealing shyness of a young man who is constantly afraid that his words won't come out just right.

The one-armed officer looked at him and smiled. 'You'll get there soon enough, never fear,' he said.

The young officer looked respectfully at the one-armed man's gaunt face, so unexpectedly lit up by a smile, fell silent and went back to preparing the tea. And indeed, the one-armed officer's face, his posture and particularly his empty greatcoat sleeve all bore witness to his calm equanimity, which could be read as saying, in any situation and any conversation, 'All this is perfectly fine, but I know it all already, and I'm capable of doing just what I please.'

'What shall we do, then?' the young officer asked his companion in the quilted kaftan. 'Shall we spend the night here, or carry on with our own horse?'

The other officer declined to go any further.

'Just imagine, Captain,' the young officer pouring out the tea went on, addressing the one-armed man and picking up the knife he had dropped, 'we were told that horses were dreadfully dear in Sevastopol, so we clubbed together and bought one in Simferopol.'

'I suppose they charged you a pretty penny, too?'

'I don't honestly know, Captain. We paid ninety roubles for the horse and the cart thrown in with it. Was that very expensive?' He directed his question to everyone around, including Kozeltsov who was watching him.

'No, that's not a lot, if it's a young horse,' said Kozeltsov.

'That's what we thought—but we were told it was a lot… Only it limps a bit, but that'll pass, they said. It's quite a tough animal.'

'Which cadet corps were you in?' asked Kozeltsov, wanting to find out about his brother.

'We've come from the Nobility Regiment—there are six of us here, we're all on the way to Sevastopol as volunteers,' replied the young officer, who clearly enjoyed talking. 'Only we don't know where the batteries are that we've been posted to—some people said they're in Sevastopol, but these people here said they're in Odessa.'

'Couldn't you have found out in Simferopol?' asked Kozeltsov.

'They don't know there… Can you imagine, one of us went to ask at an office there, and they were frightfully rude to him… can you imagine, how unpleasant of them!.. Would you like a ready-rolled cigarette of mine?' he asked the one-armed officer, who was feeling around for his cigarette-case. The young man was in a positive ecstasy of obsequious solicitude.

'And have you come from Sevastopol too?' he went on. 'Oh, my goodness, how amazing! Back in Petersburg, we never stopped thinking about you, all you heroes!' he said, addressing Kozeltsov with respectful admiration.

'So might you have to turn back again, then?' asked the lieutenant.

'That's just what we're afraid of. Just imagine, once we'd bought the horse and all the other things we needed—a coffee pot with a spirit stove, and a few other little essentials—we had no money left at all,' he concluded in a quiet voice, looking round at his companion. 'So if we do have to turn back, we've no idea how we'll manage.'

'But surely they must have given you your travel expenses?' asked Kozeltsov.

'No,' he replied in a whisper. 'They just told us they'd be paid here.'

'And do you have a certificate?'

'I know the certificate's the most important thing; but a senator in Moscow—he's my uncle, actually—well, I went to see him, and he said we'd be given a certificate here, otherwise he'd have given me one himself. So will they really give me one?'

'Oh, I'm sure they will.'

'Yes, I expect so, too,' he said, in a tone of voice that made it quite clear that he had already asked the same question at thirty other post-houses on his way, receiving a different answer every time, so that he now no longer believed anything he was told.

5

'How could he say that?' came a sudden exclamation from the officer who had been involved in the angry altercation with the postmaster on the porch, coming over to join the conversation. His words were partly addressed to the staff officers sitting nearby, whom he evidently regarded as a more worthy audience. 'Just like these gentlemen here, I had volunteered for active service, even to fight in Sevastopol, giving up a fine position, but apart from a hundred and thirty-six roubles in travelling expenses from P——, I was given nothing for the journey, and I've already spent more than a hundred and fifty of my own money. Just think of it—it's taken me almost three months to cover five hundred miles, getting on for two months in the company of these gentlemen. Just as well I brought money of my own—but supposing I hadn't?'

'Has it really taken you almost three months?' someone asked.

'What was I supposed to do?' the speaker went on. 'If I hadn't wanted to get there, I wouldn't have given up a good post and volunteered for it; so obviously I wouldn't have chosen to kill time on my way. It wasn't that I was afraid, there was just no way to get on. I had to wait two weeks at Perekop, for instance—the postmaster there wouldn't even speak to me. You just want to go when it suits you, he says, but look at all the urgent travel orders I've got here, and that's not all of them. Well, that's life, I suppose… I really did want to get on, but that's just how things turned out.

It wasn't because of the bombardment here, it was just that no matter how hard I tried to get going, it made no difference. But I was really keen to…'

The officer was taking such pains to explain his delay, and trying so hard to find excuses for it, that it was tempting to suspect that he really was afraid. This became even more obvious when he began asking where his regiment was stationed and whether it was dangerous there. He even went pale and faltered in his speech when the one-armed officer, who was from the same regiment, told him that over the past two days they had lost seventeen men from among the officers alone.

And it was perfectly true—by now, this officer had turned into an abject coward, though six months earlier he had been nothing of the kind. He had suffered the same sort of transformation that had affected many others before him, and would go on to affect many more. He had lived in one of those Russian provinces in which there are cadet corps, and had occupied a good, quiet position, until he began reading, in the newspapers and in letters from his friends, about the exploits of the heroes of Sevastopol, his former comrades—and he was suddenly inflamed with ambition and, even more, with patriotism.

He had sacrificed a great deal in the name of this emotion—his comfortable position, his little apartment with its cosy furniture, which had cost him eight years of hard work, his friends and acquaintances, and his hopes of a rich marriage. He had sacrificed all this to volunteer for active service as long ago as last February, dreaming of a wreath of deathless glory and a general's epaulettes. Two months after volunteering, he had received an official letter enquiring whether he would need financial support from the government. He replied that he would not, and went on patiently waiting for a posting, though his patriotic fervour had markedly cooled off over those two months. After another two months he received an enquiry about whether he belonged to any Masonic lodges, and other routine questions of the same sort, and replied in the negative; and finally, at the end of five months, his posting came through. But over this time he had become persuaded, partly by his friends but most of all through that underlying sense of discontent with anything new, which one always feels whenever one's situation undergoes a change, that he had made a huge mistake in volunteering for active service in the army. And then, when he found himself alone, suffering from heartburn and with his face covered in dust, at the fifth post-house, and ran into a courier from Sevastopol who told him all about the horrors of the war—and then had to wait twelve hours for a change of horses—he utterly repented of his stupid decision, began to reflect with a vague sense of terror on what awaited him, and continued on his journey in a state of numb insensibility, as though bound for the slaughter. His three months' wanderings from one post-house to the next, forced to wait at almost every one of them, and everywhere meeting with officers travelling back from Sevastopol with terrible stories to tell, had gradually increased this sense of horror, reducing this unfortunate man from a hero ready for the most desperate deeds of bravery, as he had felt himself to be at P——, to the abject coward he had become at Duvankoy. When, a month earlier, he had fallen in with the young officers who had just left the cadet corps, he tried to spin the journey out as much as he could, regarding these as the last days of his life. At every stop he would set up his camp bed, bring out his stock of provisions, and organize games of preference with the other travellers; he studied the complaints book as a way to pass the time, and rejoiced when there were no horses to be had.

If he had gone straight from P—— to the bastions, he really would have been a hero. But now he had a great deal of moral anguish to pass through before he could ever become a typical Russian officer, calm and patient in toil and danger, such as we imagine these men to be. It was not going to be easy to rekindle that enthusiasm in him.

6

'WHO ORDERED BORSCH?' called out the hostess, a fat, grubby-looking woman in her forties, coming into the room with a bowl of cabbage soup.

The conversation died away at once, and everyone in the room stared at the lady with the bowl. The officer from P—— even winked at the young officer when he looked in her direction.

'Ah, that was Kozeltsov,' said the young officer. 'We'll have to wake him. Rise and shine, dinnertime,' he said, coming up to the sleeper on the sofa and shaking him by the shoulder.

The young lad of about seventeen, with merry dark eyes and a pink flush covering his cheeks, jumped smartly up from the sofa, stepped over to the middle of the room and stood there rubbing his eyes.

'Oh, I'm so sorry,' he said in a rich, silvery voice to the doctor he had bumped into as he rose.

Lieutenant Kozeltsov recognized his brother at once, and went over to him.

'Don't you recognize me?' he asked with a smile.

'Aha-ah!' cried the younger brother. 'What a surprise!' And he embraced and kissed him.

They exchanged three kisses, but on the third one they hesitated, as if they had each had the same thought: why three kisses?

'Oh, I'm so glad to see you!' said the elder one, looking hard at his brother. 'Let's go out to the porch and talk.'

'Yes, let's. I don't want any borsch—you have it, Federson,' he said to his friend.

'Oh, but you wanted to eat, didn't you?'

'No, I don't want anything.'

Outside on the porch, the younger man kept asking his brother: 'So, how are things? Tell me how it's all going,' and repeating how glad he was to see him, without telling him anything about himself.

After five minutes on the porch, during which the conversation had flagged once or twice, the older man asked why his younger brother had not joined the Guards, as all the family had expected.

'Ah, yes!' the younger man replied, blushing at the very recollection. 'That got me down terribly—I never expected it. Can you imagine, just before our finals, three of us went off to have a smoke—you know that little room just behind the porter's lodge, surely it must have been the same in your day—but what do you think! That swine of a porter, whom we'd all tipped a number of times, saw us and ran off to tell the duty officer, who crept up on us—but as soon as we saw him, the others chucked their cigarettes and nipped out of the side door, but I wasn't quick enough, and he started making himself unpleasant to me, but I didn't stand for it. So he reported me to the inspector, and that was that. That was why I got a low mark for conduct, though all my other marks were excellent, except for a twelve for mechanics. But that was it. They discharged me to the regular army. Later they promised to transfer me to the Guards, but I didn't care any more, I asked to be sent on active service.'

'Well I never!'

'Honestly, I'm not joking—I was so fed up with everything, I wanted to get to Sevastopol as quick as I could. Actually, if everything works out now, I can do better here than if I was in the Guards—it takes you ten years to get up to colonel there, while here Totleben got from lieutenant-colonel to general in two years. And if I get killed—well, what can you do about that?'

'What a one you are!' said his brother with a smile.

'And the main thing is, brother, do you know what?' said the younger man, smiling and blushing as if he was about to come out with something very shameful. 'None of that matters—the main thing is, I volunteered because somehow you feel guilty living in Petersburg, when people here are dying for their country. And I wanted to be with you,' he added, even more shyly.

'What an odd fellow you are!' said his elder brother, getting out his cigarette case and not looking at him. 'But it's a pity we won't be together.'

'Now tell me honestly, is it really terrible on the bastions?' the younger man asked suddenly.

'It's frightening at first, but then you get used to it; it's not too bad. You'll see.'

'Tell me another thing: what do you think? Will they take Sevastopol? I don't think they can possibly take it.'

'God knows.'

'There's just one thing that annoys me—just think what bad luck—we had a whole bundle stolen from us on the way, and I had my shako in it. So now I'm in a real fix, and I've no idea how I'm going to present myself. You know we all have new-style shakos now, and they've changed lots of other things too, all of them improvements. I can tell you all about that. When I was in Moscow, I got around everywhere.'

Kozeltsov junior, whose name was Vladimir, looked very much like his brother Mikhail—but it was like the resemblance of a budding rose bush to a faded briar. He had the same chestnut hair, but it was thick, and grew in curls about his temples. Over the soft white nape of his neck, he had a little chestnut curl sticking up—our nannies say it's a sign of good luck. The skin of his face was soft and light, but it had a full-blooded youthful glow that came and went, not resting there but bursting out from time to time, reflecting every shift of his thoughts. He had his brother's eyes, but his own were brighter and more open, a feature that was all the more marked because they were often overlaid by a fine film of moisture. There was a light, tawny down on his cheeks and upper lip; his pink lips often creased in a shy smile to reveal his shiny white teeth. Well built and broad shouldered, in an unbuttoned greatcoat revealing a red shirt with a collar buttoned at the side, holding a cigarette between his fingers and resting his elbows on the porch balustrade, he stood facing his brother with innocent joy in his face and in every gesture—such a pleasant, good-looking boy that anyone would have been happy just to gaze at him. He was overjoyed to see his brother again, and kept looking at him with pride and respect, imagining him a hero. And yet in some respects, particularly regarding his social polish (though he himself was also lacking in this), his ability to speak French, to conduct himself correctly in the presence of important people, to dance, and so forth—he was slightly ashamed of his older brother, looked down on him and would even have liked to educate him. His head was still full of Petersburg, and particularly of the home of a certain lady who liked handsome young boys and used to invite him round on festive occasions; full, too, of the Moscow residence of a senator, where he had once danced at a grand ball.

7

WHEN THEY HAD said almost all there was to be said, and had begun to feel as one often does on such occasions—that although they were fond of each other, they really had little in common—the brothers stayed silent for quite a while.

'Well, get your things and let's be off at once,' said the older one at last.

His brother suddenly blushed and hesitated.

'You mean straight to Sevastopol?' he asked after a silence.

'Yes, why not—you haven't got much with you, have you? I think we can get it all in.'

'Splendid! Yes, let's go at once,' said the younger man with a sigh, and set off for the saloon. But without opening the door, he stopped before it, hung his head sadly, and began thinking.

'Straight to Sevastopol, right now, that hellhole—horrible! Still, it can't be helped, it had to happen sometime. Now at least I'll be with my brother...'

The fact was that it was only now, at the thought that once he took his place in the cart, he would find himself in Sevastopol before he got out again, and that no chance event could hold him up any more, that he suddenly had a clear picture in his mind of the danger he had been seeking—and he lost heart, and felt afraid at the very thought of how close it was. Somehow he pulled himself together and went indoors; but a quarter of an hour passed, and still he had not rejoined his brother. The older man eventually opened the door himself, to call his brother out. The younger Kozeltsov, holding himself like a guilty schoolboy, was talking about something with the officer from P——. When his brother opened the door, he did not know where to look.

'Just coming, I'll be out in a second,' he said, gesturing to his brother to go out again. 'Wait for me outside.'

A minute later he really did come out, and went to his brother breathing a deep sigh.

'Would you believe it—I can't go with you after all, brother,' he said.

'What? What nonsense!'

'I'll tell you the whole truth, Misha. None of us has any money left, and we all owe money to that staff captain who has come from P——. It's terribly embarrassing!'

The older brother frowned and said nothing for a long time.

'Do you owe a lot?' he asked, giving his brother a lowering look.

'A lot... well, no, not all that much; but I feel terribly ashamed of myself. He paid my account at three of the post-houses we stopped at, and we kept using his sugar... so I really don't know... oh, and we played preference too... so I do owe him something now.'

'That's not good, Volodya! Just think, what would you have done if you hadn't met me?' he demanded sternly, without looking at his younger brother.

'Well, I'd been thinking I'd pay him back when I got my expenses paid in Sevastopol. I could have done that, you know. But I'd better stay here, and get there with him tomorrow.'

His elder brother got out his purse and, with fingers that trembled a little, extracted two ten-rouble notes and one three-rouble one.

'This is all the money I've got,' he said. 'How much do you owe?'

When he said that this was all the money he possessed, Kozeltsov was not being entirely truthful. He also had four gold roubles, sewn into his lapel in case of emergencies; but he had promised himself not to touch them on any account.

It turned out that Kozeltsov junior, what with his games of preference and the sugar, only owed the officer from P—— eight roubles. His elder brother gave him the money, merely remarking that this was no way to carry on, and that if one has no money one should not play preference.

'What stakes were you playing for?'

His younger brother said not a word. His brother's question struck him as an aspersion on his honesty. He was cross with himself, ashamed of behaving in a way that could arouse such suspicions, and offended with his brother whom he loved so dearly; and all these feelings had such a powerful and painful effect on his impressionable nature that he could not bring himself to answer, feeling that he would not be able to control the tearful sobs that rose to his throat. He took the money without looking at it, and went back to his companions.

8

NIKOLAEV HAD FORTIFIED himself at Duvankoy with two jugs of vodka which he had bought from a soldier who was selling it on the bridge. Now he gave the reins a tug and the cart set off, jolting up and down along the stony road, with its patches of shade here and there, that followed the course of the Belbek towards Sevastopol. The brothers sat in the back, their legs knocking together, and although they never stopped thinking about one another, they maintained a stubborn silence.

'Why did he have to insult me?' thought the younger one. 'Couldn't he simply have said nothing about it? It's just as if he regarded me as a thief—and now he seems to be angry with me, so we'll have quarrelled for good. But how splendid it would have been to be in Sevastopol together! Two brothers, good friends with each other, fighting the enemy side by side—one of them older, though not much of a man of the world, but a brave fighter, and the other—still young, but also a splendid fellow… By the time the week was out, I'd have shown them all that I'm not as young as all that! And I'll have stopped blushing, I'll have courage in my face, and a moustache too—not a big one, but in a week it'll have grown to a decent size…' and he tweaked the downy hairs that had grown at the corners of his mouth. 'Perhaps we'll get there today, and my brother and I will find ourselves in action straight away. He must be a resolute man, very brave—the kind who doesn't say much, but puts up a better show than the others.

I wonder,' he went on, 'whether he's squeezing me against the edge of the cart like this on purpose? He probably realizes that I'm uncomfortable, and is pretending not to notice that I'm here. So we'll arrive today,' he carried on in his mind, pressing himself up against the edge of the cart, doing his best not to move a muscle for fear that his brother might notice he was uncomfortable, 'and we'll be sent straight to the bastion; I'll be helping to man the guns, and he'll go to join his company; we'll go out together. But suddenly the French charge at us. I fire and fire at them, and kill a huge number of them, but still they keep on charging at me. I can't fire any more, and of course I'm beyond help—but suddenly my brother rushes out, brandishing his sabre, I snatch up a musket, and we charge on with the other soldiers. The French hurl themselves at my brother. I rush up, kill one Frenchman, and another one, and save my brother. I'm wounded in the arm, but I shift the musket to the other arm, and carry on running. But now my brother is killed by a bullet at my side. I stop for an instant, gaze at him sadly, then get up and shout 'Follow me! Let's avenge him! I loved my brother more than anyone in the world,' I'll say, 'and now I've lost him. Let's avenge him, destroy the enemy, or all die here!' Everyone yells and they all rush after me. Now the whole French force comes out, led by Pélissier himself. We slaughter them all, but in the end I'm wounded a second time, and a third, and I fall mortally wounded. Then they all come running to me. Gorchakov will come, and ask me if I want anything. I'll tell him I don't want anything, except to be laid by my brother's side. I want to die beside him. They'll carry me and lay me down beside the bloody corpse of my brother. I'll raise myself up, and just say: "Yes, you never appreciated these two men who sincerely loved their country. Now they have both fallen… may God forgive you!" And on those words, I'll die.'

Who can say how true those words may prove to be?

'I say, have you ever been in a skirmish?' he suddenly asked his brother, completely forgetting that he had not meant to talk to him.

'No, not once,' the elder brother replied. 'We lost two thousand men from our regiment, all working on the earthworks. And I got my wound on the earthworks too. Wars aren't fought in the least the way you imagine, Volodya!'

Being called 'Volodya' touched the younger man, and he wanted to have things out with his brother, who had not the faintest idea that he had offended him.

'You're not angry with me, are you, Misha?' he asked after a moment's silence.

'Whatever for?'

'No, nothing. Just... what we were saying. No, never mind.'

'Not in the least,' said his elder brother, turning to him and slapping him on the leg.

'Well, Misha, I beg your pardon if I annoyed you.'

And the younger brother turned away to hide the tears that suddenly filled his eyes.

9

'IS THAT REALLY Sevastopol already?' asked the younger brother when they reached the top of a hill. Spread out before them lay the bay with all the ships' masts rising out of it, the open sea with the enemy fleet in the distance, the white shore batteries, barrack huts, aqueducts, the docks and town buildings, and the clouds of white and lilac-tinted smoke constantly rising over the yellow hills around the town and hanging in the blue sky, bathed in the rosy beams of the sun as it sank towards the horizon and sent flashes of reflected sunlight off the dark sea.

Volodya looked at this dreadful place, which had been so much in his thoughts, without the least shiver of fear. On the contrary, he found an aesthetic pleasure in contemplating the truly splendid, unique view, together with a heroic sense of self-satisfaction at the thought that he, too, would be there in half an hour. He went on gazing at it with concentrated attention from that moment until they finally arrived at the North Side and reached the baggage train of his brother's regiment. Here they would be able to get definite information about the regiment's location and its battery.

The officer in charge of the baggage train lived not far from what was known as the 'new town', a collection of wooden huts erected by the sailors' families, in a tent connected to a fairly large shed constructed from green oak branches that had not yet dried out completely.

The brothers found this officer sitting at a folding table, on which stood a glass of cold tea with cigarette ash floating in it, and a tray bearing a bottle of vodka and some breadcrumbs and bits of dried caviar. In his shirtsleeves, wearing a shirt of a dirty yellow colour and trousers, he was counting a huge pile of banknotes on a large abacus. But before we say anything about the officer himself or the brothers' conversation with him, we must take a closer look at the interior of this shed, and discover at least a little about the officer's occupation and way of life.

The newly constructed shed was very large, tightly woven and comfortably arranged inside, to a standard normally reserved for generals and regimental commanders, and furnished with wattle-and-turf tables and benches. To prevent leaves from falling inside, the walls and roof were hung with three carpets, very ugly but new and no doubt expensive. Below the main carpet, with its picture of a lady on horseback, was an iron bedspread covered by a bright-red plush bedspread, on which lay a torn and dirty leather cushion and a raccoon fur coat. On a nearby table were a looking-glass in a silver frame, a shockingly dirty silver hairbrush, a broken horn comb, its teeth clogged with greasy hairs, a silver candlestick, a liqueur bottle with a red and gold label, a gold watch with a portrait of Peter the Great, two gold rings, a box filled with some sort of capsules, a crust of bread, and a scattering of old playing cards. Under the bed lay several porter bottles, both full and empty.

This officer was in charge of the regiment's baggage train and the fodder for the horses. He shared his accommodation with his great friend, a commission agent who was involved in some sort of dealings on the side. When the brothers arrived, this man was asleep in the tent, while the baggage train officer was doing the regimental accounts in time for the end of the month. This officer was a handsome, soldierly-looking man—tall, with a large moustache and a well-bred, stocky build. His only unattractive features were a kind of sweaty puffiness about the face, almost hiding his little grey eyes—as though he had been bodily filled up with porter—and his extreme physical uncleanliness, ranging from his wispy, greasy hair to his big bare feet in some sort of ermine slippers.

'Just look at all that money!' exclaimed Kozeltsov senior as he entered the shed, staring hungrily at the pile of banknotes. 'You might lend me just half of that, Vasily Mikhailich!'

The baggage train officer cringed at the sight of his visitor, as though caught in the act of stealing. Gathering the money together, he bowed without rising from his seat.

'Ah, if only it was mine… Government money, my friend! And who's this you've brought with you?' he asked, putting the money away into a strongbox beside him and fixing his eyes on Volodya.

'This is my brother, straight from cadet corps. We've just dropped in to find out where our regiment is stationed.'

'Sit down, gentlemen,' the officer replied, getting up and going out into the tent, seemingly ignoring his visitors. 'Would you like anything to drink? What about some porter?' he called from there.

'That wouldn't hurt, Vasily Mikhailich!'

Volodya was impressed with the baggage train officer's grand, negligent manner, and the respect with which his brother treated him.

'He must be one of their crack officers, whom they all admire; a plain, blunt man, no doubt, but very brave and hospitable,' he thought, sitting down on the divan in a shy, self-effacing way.

'So where's your regiment stationed?' the elder brother asked into the tent.

'What's that?'

He repeated his question.

'Zeyfer was here today; he said they transferred to the fifth bastion yesterday.'

'Is that definite?'

'If I'm telling you, that means it's definite. Although actually, the devil only knows! It wouldn't take much to make him tell a lie. Well, will you have some porter?' the baggage train officer asked, still in the tent.

'Actually, I think I will,' said Kozeltsov.

'What about you, Osip Ignatich?' the voice in the tent went on, evidently addressing the commission agent who had been asleep there. 'Time to wake up, it's gone seven o'clock.'

'Stop aggravating me! I'm not asleep,' replied a thin, languid little voice, attractively slurring the letters 'l' and 'r'.

'Well, come on, get up. It's boring without you.'

And the baggage train officer came out to rejoin his visitors.

'Bring us some porter! Simferopol porter!' he shouted.

An orderly came into the shed, with what seemed to Volodya a supercilious expression, and brought out a bottle of porter from beneath Volodya's legs, jostling him as he did so.

'Yes, my friend,' said the baggage train officer, pouring out their glasses, 'we've got a new regimental commander now. He needs money, lots of it—he's buying up everything you can think of.'

'Well, I suppose he's one of the new generation, with his own ideas about everything,' said Kozeltsov, politely accepting his glass.

'The new generation, indeed! He'll be just as much of a skinflint as all the others. When he commanded a battalion, he never stopped shouting, but now he's changed his tune. It won't do, you know, lad.'

'You're right there.'

The younger brother had no idea what they were talking about, but he had a vague impression that his brother was not being quite open with the other man, merely saying things to keep him happy, since he was drinking his porter.

The bottle of porter was soon emptied, and the conversation had gone on in the same vein for some time when the tent flaps were flung aside to admit a rather short, fresh-faced man in a dark-blue satin dressing gown with tassels, and an army cap with a red band and a cockade. He emerged into the room, fingering his black moustache, and responded to the officers' bows with a barely perceptible movement of one shoulder while fixing his eyes on some spot on the carpet.

'I'll have a glass too, if I may!' he said, sitting down at the table. 'Well now, young man, you've just arrived from Petersburg, have you?' he asked Volodya in a friendly tone.

'Yes, sir, on my way to Sevastopol.'

'Volunteered, did you?'

'Yes, sir.'

'I don't know what gets into you gentlemen, I really don't!' the commission agent went on. 'By now, I think I'd be happy to go back to Petersburg on foot, if they'd let me. God knows I'm sick and tired of this dog's life we lead here!'

'What's so bad about it?' demanded Kozeltsov. 'You seem to have a pretty nice life here!' The commission agent gave him a look and turned away.

'It's this constant danger' ('What danger can he mean, sitting over here on the North Side?' wondered Kozeltsov), 'the deprivation, you can't get hold of anything,' he went on, still addressing Volodya. 'And what makes you want to come here—honest to goodness, I don't understand you gentlemen! If there was anything in it for you—but there's nothing, and you still come here. What good will it do you, at your age, if you suddenly find yourself a cripple for life?'

'Some people are out for profit, while others serve for their honour's sake!' Kozeltsov senior broke in again, with annoyance in his voice.

'What's the use of honour when there's nothing to eat!' retorted the commission agent with a derisive laugh, turning to the baggage train officer, who also laughed. 'Play us a bit of "Lucia",* and we'll listen to that,' he went on, pointing to a musical box, 'I just love it.'

'What's he like—is he a good chap, that Vasily Mikhailich?' Volodya asked his brother when they emerged from the shed as dusk was falling to continue their journey to Sevastopol.

'He's all right, but such a tight-fisted wretch, it's a disgrace! He makes not less than three hundred roubles a month, and yet he lives like a pig, as you saw. But that commission agent, I can't stand him—sooner or later I'll give him a thrashing. You know, that swine arrived here from Turkey with twelve thousand...' And Kozeltsov launched into an account of the man's peculation, partly (if the truth be told) with that special annoyance of a man whose condemnation rests not so much on the fact that peculation is bad, as on his resentment that other people do well by it.

---

* 'Santa Lucia', a traditional Neapolitan-language song first published in Italian translation in 1849.

10

When they approached the big pontoon bridge across the bay, almost at nightfall, Volodya was not precisely in a bad mood, but he was feeling a certain heaviness of heart. All he had seen and heard was so out of keeping with his impressions of the recent past—the spacious, brightly lit examination hall with its parquet floor, his friends' merry, good-natured voices and laughter, his new uniform, his beloved Tsar whom he had got used to seeing over the past seven years, and who, bidding them farewell with tears in his eyes, had called them his children—everything he was seeing now was so unlike those beautiful, glorious, rainbow-coloured dreams.

'Well, so here we are!' said his elder brother when they reached the Mikhailov battery and got out of the waggon. 'If they let us cross the bridge we'll go straight to the Nikolaev barracks. You can stay there overnight, while I go to my regiment and find out where your battery is stationed. Then I'll pick you up tomorrow.'

'What for? Why not just go together?' said Volodya. 'And I'll go to the bastion with you too. I mean, it makes no difference—I've got to get used to it. If you can go, then so can I.'

'Better not.'

'No, please let me—at least I'll find out how…'

'I'm advising you not to come, but if you insist…'

The sky was dark and cloudless; the stars, the lights of one flying mortar bomb after another, and the gunfire were already lighting up the gloom. The large white structure of the battery and the near end of the bridge loomed in the darkness. Literally every second the air was shaken, ever more loudly and distinctly, by the noise of cannon shots and explosions, coming simultaneously or in quick succession. Through this noise, and seeming to echo it, one could hear the dull rumble of the bay. A breeze was blowing in from the sea, and the air smelt damp. The brothers approached the bridge. A militiaman clattered his musket clumsily against the ground as he raised it and shouted:

'Who goes there?'

'Soldiers!'

'I've orders to let nobody pass.'

'Come on! We've got to.'

'Speak to the officer.'

An officer, sitting dozing on an anchor nearby, raised himself and ordered the brothers to be let through.

'You can go across, but you can't come back. Hey, what are you doing, pushing through all at once!' he yelled at the regimental waggons piled high with gabions, which were crowding at the entrance.

Stepping down onto the first pontoon, the brothers ran into some soldiers coming from the other side, talking loudly to each other.

'If he's had his ammunition money, then he's squared his accounts in full—that's what…'

'Hey, lads!' said another voice, 'When you get over to the North Side, that's the real world, by God it is! The air's completely different.'

'You're joking!' said the first. 'Only the other day one of those damned things came flying over there and blew the legs clean off two of our sailors. So none of that talk here!'

The brothers walked across the first pontoon, waiting for the waggon to arrive, and stopped on the second which was already shipping water here and there. The wind, which had felt gentle when they were ashore, had become very strong and gusty here; the pontoon bridge was rocking in the water, and the waves, beating noisily against the timbers and breaking up against the anchors and cables, were flooding the planks. To their right was the howling sea, black, misty and menacing, with a continuous smooth black line marking it off from the starry skyline with its blend of greyness and pallor, and the lights of the enemy fleet gleaming in the far distance; to their left was the black mass of a Russian ship, and the sound of the waves beating against its side. A steamer could be seen puffing noisily away from the North Side. The flash of a bomb bursting close by it briefly lit up the tall piles of gabions on its deck, two men standing on the upper deck, and the white foam and spray from the greenish waves thrown up by the ship as it ploughed through them. By the edge of the pontoon bridge sat a man in shirtsleeves, dangling his legs in the water and repairing something on the bridge. Ahead of them, in the sky over Sevastopol, there were more of the same flashes of light, and the dreadful sounds were carried towards them louder and louder. A wave coming in from the sea broke against the right side of the bridge, drenching Volodya's legs. Two soldiers came splashing through the water past him. Suddenly something burst with a crash above them, lighting up the bridge, a waggon driving across it, and a man on horseback; bomb fragments hissed through the air and raised fountains of spray as they hit the water.

'Ah, Mikhail Semyonich!' said the rider, reining in his horse in front of the elder Kozeltsov, 'Quite recovered, then?'

'As you see. Where are you off to?'

'The North Side, to get more ammunition. I'm standing in for the regimental adjutant today—we're expecting an assault any moment, and we've barely got five rounds per man. What a mess!'

'And where's Martsov?'

'Got his leg blown off yesterday... Sleeping in his room, in town... You might find him, he's at the dressing station.'

'The regiment's on the fifth bastion, right?'

'Yes, we've relieved the M—— regiment there. Do look in to the dressing station, you'll find some of our lot there, they'll take you across.'

'Well, and is my room on the Morskaya still in one piece?'

'Oh, my dear chap! Smashed to rubble long ago. You wouldn't know Sevastopol any more—not a woman left in the place, no taverns, no music—the last bar closed down yesterday. It's all really miserable there now... Goodbye!'

And the officer rode off at a fast trot.

Volodya suddenly felt terribly afraid—he could not shake off the feeling that a cannonball or a bomb fragment was about to land on his head at any moment. The damp gloom, all those noises, especially the growling splash of the waves... everything seemed to be telling him to go no further, that no good awaited him here, that he would never again set foot on Russian soil on this side of the bay, and that he ought to turn back at once and run away as far as he could from this terrible place of death. 'But perhaps it's already too late, perhaps it's all decided by now,' he thought, shivering partly at this thought and partly because the water had soaked through his boots and his feet were wet.

He heaved a deep sigh, and walked a little way off from his brother.

'My God! Am I really going to get killed then, me of all people? Oh Lord, have mercy on me!' he whispered, and crossed himself.

'Let's go then, Volodya,' said his elder brother, when the cart had rolled onto the bridge. 'Did you see that mortar bomb?'

On the bridge the brothers met other carts loaded with wounded men, or with gabions; one cart, driven by a woman, was carrying furniture. On the far shore, no one stopped them. Following their instinct and keeping close to the wall of the Nikolaev battery, the brothers walked silently along, listening to the bombs exploding, right overhead now, and the roar of the fragments as they showered down; and at last reached the place on the battery where the icon was placed. Here they were told that the 5th light battery, to which Volodya had been assigned, was stationed on the Korabelnaya; so they agreed together that in spite of the danger, they would spend the night at the elder brother's quarters on the fifth bastion, and carry on to the battery next day. Entering a passage, they picked their way over the legs of sleeping soldiers lying along the whole length of the battery wall, and at last reached the dressing station.

11

THEY CAME INTO the first ward, where wounded men were lying on camp beds. The air in the room was heavy with that repulsive sickly smell of hospitals. Here they were met by two Sisters of Mercy who came out to receive them.

One was a woman aged about fifty, with dark eyes and a severe expression, carrying a pile of lint and bandages. She was issuing instructions to a young medical attendant, who was following her around. The other was a very pretty girl of twenty, with a pale, delicate, fair-complexioned face who looked out from under the white cap that framed her head with a sweet and somehow helpless expression. She walked beside the older woman with lowered eyes, hands in her apron pockets, and seemed to be scared of falling behind.

Kozeltsov asked them whether they knew where Martsov could be found—a man who had had his leg blown off the day before.

'From the P—— regiment, isn't he?' asked the older nurse. 'Is he a relative of yours?'

'No, ma'am, a friend.'

'Hmm! Take them along,' she said in French to the younger nurse. 'It's that way.' And she and the medical assistant went over to another wounded man.

'Do come along! What are you staring at?' Kozeltsov asked Volodya, who was standing with a wide-eyed, agonized expression, unable to take his eyes off the wounded men. 'Come along!'

Volodya went out with his brother, but kept looking round and unconsciously repeating:

'Oh my God! Oh my God!'

'Hasn't been here long, I suppose?' the nurse asked Kozeltsov, indicating Volodya who was following them down the corridor, sighing and groaning.

'Just got here.'

The pretty nurse looked at Volodya and suddenly started crying.

'Oh God, oh God, when's it all going to end?' she exclaimed with despair in her voice.

They went into the officers' ward. Martsov was lying on his back, his sinewy arms, bare to the elbow, behind his head; his yellow-tinged face had the expression of someone clenching his teeth so as not to cry out with pain. His uninjured leg in its stocking was thrust out from under the blanket, and his toes could be seen twitching convulsively.

'Well, how are you doing?' asked the nurse, lifting his balding head with her gentle, slender fingers, on one of which Volodya noticed a gold ring, and straightening his pillow. 'Here are your friends, come to see you.'

'It's hurting, obviously,' he answered irritably. 'Leave me alone, I'm all right!' And the toes inside the stocking twitched harder still. 'Hello! Excuse me, but what's your name?' he asked Kozeltsov. 'Oh yes, I'm sorry, one forgets everything here,' he said when Kozeltsov told him. 'We used to share the same quarters, didn't we?' he added without any particular pleasure, and then looked enquiringly at Volodya.

'That's my brother, he's just arrived from Petersburg.'

'Hmm! Well, I've earned myself a full discharge,' he said, wincing. 'Ow, that really hurts!.. The best thing would be a quick end to it all.'

He gave his leg a jerk, muttered something and covered his face in his hands.

'You have to leave him,' the nurse whispered, with tears in her eyes. 'He's in a very bad way.'

Back on the North Side, the brothers had decided to go to the fifth bastion together; but when they left the Nikolaev battery, they seemed to have silently agreed not to expose themselves to unnecessary dangers. Without saying a word on the subject, they decided to go their separate ways.

'Only how are you going to find your way, Volodya?' asked the elder brother. 'I suppose Nikolaev will take you over to Korabelnaya; I'll go off on my own now and be with you again tomorrow.'

Nothing else was said between the two brothers during this, their last farewell.

12

THE THUNDEROUS CANNON FIRE continued unabated, but Catherine Street, as Volodya walked along it with the taciturn Nikolaev following behind him, was silent and deserted. All he could make out in the darkness was a wide street with the white walls of large houses, many of them reduced to rubble, and the stone pavement along which he was walking. Now and then he encountered soldiers or officers. Passing along the left-hand side of the street, near the Admiralty, the light of a bright lamp burning beyond a wall lit up the acacias planted along the pavement, with their green supports and pitiful dusty leaves. He heard the very clear sound of his own footsteps and those of Nikolaev, following behind him and breathing heavily. He was not thinking of anything in particular; the pretty nurse, Martsov's leg with his toes moving inside his stocking, the darkness, the bombs, and all kinds of images of death drifted vaguely through his mind. His young, impressionable soul ached and shrank from the knowledge of how lonely he felt and how indifferent everyone was to his fate, in his hour of danger. 'I'll be killed, I'll suffer agonies of pain, and no one will shed a tear for me!' All this had come upon him instead of the hero's life, full of energy and surrounded by fellow feeling, that he had been so fondly imagining. Bombs whistled about him, bursting closer and closer; Nikolaev heaved sigh after sigh, but said nothing to break the silence. As they crossed the bridge to Korabelnaya, he saw something fly hissing past him to land in the bay not far off. For a second it cast a crimson light over the lilac waves, then vanished only to rise out of the sea again in a shower of spray.

'Look at that—still alight!' said Nikolaev.

'Yes,' he answered, startled to hear his unexpectedly thin, feeble, piping voice.

They were met by stretcher bearers carrying wounded men, and more regimental transports with gabions; on the Korabelnaya they passed some nameless regiment, and some mounted men rode by. One of them was an officer accompanied by a Cossack. He was riding at a fast trot, but at the sight of Volodya he drew up beside him, stared at his face, turned away and rode off, giving his horse a crack of the whip. 'Alone, alone! Nobody cares whether I'm here on this earth or not,' thought the poor boy with horror. He felt genuinely close to bursting into tears.

Going on uphill past a high white wall, he found himself in a street of little devastated houses, constantly lit up by exploding bombs. A drunk, dishevelled woman coming out of a gate with a sailor ran into him.

''Cause if he'd been a decent bloke…' she mumbled, 'oh, begging your pardon, your Honour, Officer!'

The poor lad's heart sank deeper and deeper; the lightning flashes came thicker and faster on the black horizon, and the bombs whistled over his head closer and closer together, to fall and explode nearby. Nikolaev heaved a deep sigh and suddenly began to speak in a voice that seemed to Volodya to come from somewhere beyond the grave:

'There he was, in such a hurry to leave home. Riding on and on! What was all the hurry to get here? A gentleman with any sense, soon as he's got the slightest wound, he's off to hospital and there he stays! That's the only sensible thing to do.'

'What do you mean? When my brother's quite well again now,' said Volodya, hoping that some conversation might dispel the black mood that had come over him.

'Well, indeed! What do you mean, he's well, when he's still as sick as anything? And even the ones who really are well, if they've got any sense, stay put in hospital at a time like this. Not much fun out here, now, is it! You'll get your leg blown off, or your arm, and that's your lot! And it won't be long before it happens, either! It's bad enough here in town, but up on those bastions it'll be far worse. You walk along and all you can do is say prayers to yourself. Look at that devil up there, screaming past us!' he added, drawing Volodya's attention to the sound of a bomb fragment whizzing through the air. 'Right now,' Nikolaev went on, 'he ordered me to show your Honour the way. Well, we know orders are orders, and I've got to do as I'm told; but the main thing is, he's left the cart with some soldier or other, and the bundle's untied. So off I go, because he says so; but when something goes missing, it'll be Nikolaev's fault, you'll see!'

A few steps further on they emerged onto a square. Nikolaev sighed in silence.

'There's your artillery over there, your Honour!' he said abruptly. 'Ask that sentry, he'll show you where to go.' And when Volodya had gone on a little further, he could no longer hear Nikolaev sighing behind him.

All at once he felt utterly, hopelessly alone. The feeling that he had been abandoned on his own in the face of danger—waiting to be killed, as he felt—settled on his heart like a cold and crushingly heavy stone. He stopped in the middle of the square and looked round to see if anyone was watching him, clutched at his head and thought out loud, filled with horror: 'Oh Lord! Am I really a coward, a vile, despicable, worthless coward? Can't I die an honourable death for my country, for my Tsar, when I was dreaming so joyfully of dying for him such a short while ago? No! I'm a pathetic, wretched creature!' And with his heart filled with a real sense of despair and disillusionment with himself, Volodya asked the sentry the way to the battery commander's quarters, and went the way he was told.

13

THE BATTERY COMMANDER's house to which the sentry had directed him was a small two-storey house with its entrance in a courtyard. The dim light of a candle shone through one of the windows, which was pasted over with paper. An orderly was sitting in the porch, smoking a pipe. He went in to report Volodya's arrival to the commander, and showed Volodya into a room which contained two windows with a desk between them, under a broken mirror. The table was littered with official papers. There were also a few chairs, an iron bed with clean bedding and a little rug on the floor beside it.

Beside the door stood a handsome man with a large moustache—a sergeant-major in a greatcoat, with a broadsword on his belt and a St George Cross and Hungarian Medal on his chest. Behind him, in the middle of the room, a short staff officer aged about forty in a thin, worn old greatcoat was pacing to and fro; one of his cheeks was swollen and tied in a bandage.

'Beg to report, sir, Ensign Kozeltsov II, posted to the 5th light battery,' Volodya recited the phrase he had learnt as a cadet, on entering the room.

The battery commander curtly returned his bow without offering his hand, and invited him to sit down.

Volodya lowered himself timidly onto the chair by the writing desk and began fiddling with a pair of scissors that had somehow found their way into his hands. The battery commander went on walking silently back and forth across the room, head down and hands behind his back, only now and then glancing at those hands playing with the scissors. He looked as if he was in the middle of remembering something.

He was a rather stout little man with a big bald patch on the crown of his head, a thick moustache which grew straight down and covered his mouth, and large, pleasant eyes. He had fine, clean, plump hands; his toes turned out markedly, and he walked with a confident and slightly foppish gait, demonstrating that this battery commander was no shrinking violet.

'Yes,' he said, stopping in front of the sergeant-major, 'we'll have to start giving those ammunition horses extra fodder tomorrow, they're getting too thin. What do you think?'

'Yes, we could give them a bit extra, why not, your Honour! Oats have got cheaper right now,' the sergeant-major replied, with a movement of his fingers which he still kept firmly by the seams of his trousers, but which he evidently liked to use for gesturing as he spoke. 'And another thing, your Honour—our forager Franschuk sent me a note from the baggage train yesterday to say that we absolutely must buy some axles there—apparently they're cheap now. So what would you like me to do, sir?'

'All right, tell him to buy some—he's got the money, after all.' The battery commander began pacing across the room again. 'Where's your kit?' he asked Volodya abruptly, stopping in front of him.

Poor Volodya was so oppressed by the thought that he was a coward that he saw contempt for his pathetic cowardice in every look and every word addressed to him. He felt that the battery commander had already seen through his secret, and was making fun of him. Covered in confusion, he replied that his kit was on the Grafskaya and his brother had promised to deliver it to him next day.

But the lieutenant-colonel did not hear him out. Turning to the sergeant-major, he asked:

'Where are we going to put this ensign?'

'Ensign, sir?' said the sergeant-major, further embarrassing Volodya by his cursory glance, which seemed to say 'What sort of an ensign is this, and is it worth putting him anywhere?' — 'Why not downstairs, your Honour, in the staff captain's quarters,' he said after a moment's thought — 'the staff captain's out on the bastion at present, so this gentleman could have his bed.'

'So there you are—will that do for you tonight?' asked the battery commander. 'I dare say you're tired now; we'll find something better for you tomorrow.'

Volodya stood up and bowed.

'Wouldn't you like some tea?' asked the battery commander as Volodya approached the door. 'We could light the samovar.'

Volodya bowed and went out. The lieutenant-colonel's orderly escorted him downstairs and showed him into a bare, dirty room littered with all sorts of stuff lying around, and an iron bedstead with no bedding or blankets. Lying asleep on the bed, covered by a heavy greatcoat, was a man in a pink shirt. Volodya thought at first that he was just a soldier.

'Pyotr Nikolayich!' said the orderly, shaking him by the shoulder. 'Here's an ensign come to sleep here… This is our cadet,' he added to the ensign.

'Oh, don't bother, please!' said Volodya. But the cadet, a tall, stout young man with a handsome but very stupid-looking face, got up from the bed, threw his greatcoat over his shoulders, and left the room, evidently still half asleep.

'It's all right,' he muttered, 'I'll lie down outside.'

14

LEFT ALONE with his thoughts, Volodya's first impulse was one of revulsion against the chaotic, cheerless state of his own mind. He longed to fall asleep and forget everything around him—and above all, to forget himself. He snuffed out his candle, took off his greatcoat and lay down on the bed, covering his whole body and head with the greatcoat to shut out his fear of the dark, from which he had suffered since childhood. But suddenly it occurred to him that a bomb might come flying over, smash through the roof and kill him. He started listening. Right above his head he could hear the battery commander's footsteps.

'Well, even if a bomb does fall,' he thought, 'it'll kill whoever's upstairs first, and then me. So at least I won't be the only one.' That thought gave him some comfort, and he began to nod off. 'But supposing Sevastopol is captured in the night, and the French break in here? What can I use to defend myself?' He got up again and walked round the room. His fear of genuine danger drove away his superstitious fear of the dark. Apart from a saddle and a samovar, there was nothing solid in the room. 'I'm hopeless, I'm a coward, a vile coward!' he suddenly thought, and came back to his oppressive feeling of self-contempt and even revulsion. He lay down again and tried not to think. But he could not stop the impressions of that day from rising up in his mind once more, echoed by the incessant noise of the bombardment which made the glass rattle in the single window of the room. That noise reminded him of the danger he was in; he had visions of wounded men, and blood, or bombs and fragments flying into the room, or the pretty nurse bandaging him and weeping over him as he lay dying, or his mother coming to see him off in the local town and praying fervently and tearfully before a miraculous icon—and once again, sleep seemed impossible. But suddenly he had a clear and distinct thought of an almighty, benevolent God, who could make anything happen and who heard every prayer. He knelt down, crossed himself and folded his hands as he had been taught as a child when he prayed. And that gesture suddenly transported him to a long-forgotten state of serene consolation.

'If I have to die—if I must cease to exist—then make it happen, O Lord,' he thought, 'make it happen quickly. But if what is needed is courage, and fortitude, which I do not have—then grant me them, and save me from shame and disgrace which I cannot bear, and teach me what I must do to carry out your will.'

His childlike, frightened, circumscribed soul suddenly grew braver and brighter, and his eyes were opened to new, expansive, radiant horizons. He lived through a great many more thoughts and feelings in the short time that this feeling lasted, but soon fell into a calm, untroubled sleep, to the continued crashing of the bombardment and rattling of the windowpanes.

Almighty God! You alone have heard, you alone know those simple but ardent and despairing prayers of ignorance, of troubled repentance and suffering, that have ascended to you from this terrible place of death—whether from the general who only a moment ago had been thinking of his lunch and a St George Cross round his neck, but was now suffering with a dread sense of your closeness; or from the exhausted, famished, louse-ridden soldier lying sprawled on the bare floor of the Nikolaev battery, begging you to grant him quickly the reward he unconsciously looks to, which will make up for all his undeserved sufferings. Truly, you never tire of hearkening to the prayers of your children; wherever they are, you send them your angel of comfort, to fill their souls with patience, the sense of duty, and the consolation of hope.

15

THE ELDER KOZELTSOV, meeting a soldier from his own regiment in the street, went directly to the fifth bastion with him.

'Keep close to the wall, your Honour!' said the soldier.

'What for?'

'It's dangerous, your Honour; there it goes, straight over our heads,' said the soldier, listening to the whistle of a cannonball as it flew past, to strike the dry roadway across the street.

Taking no notice of the man, Kozeltsov strode briskly down the middle of the road.

These were the same streets as in the springtime, when he had last been in Sevastopol; the same flashes—perhaps even more frequent now; the same sounds, and groans, and encounters with wounded men; and the same batteries, earthworks and trenches. But all this seemed somehow more melancholy now, and at the same time more intense—more shot holes in the walls, no lights in the windows any more, except for the ones in the Kuschin house (which was the hospital); not one woman to be seen anywhere. Instead of the old feeling that this was something one had got used to and no longer worried about, there was now a sense of anxious expectation, weariness and tension.

Here was the last trench, and here was the voice of some private from the P—— regiment who recognized his old company commander; here was the 3rd battalion waiting in the darkness, huddled up against a wall, lit up now and then by gunshots, with the muffled sounds of talk and the clatter of muskets.

'Where's the regimental commander?' Kozeltsov asked.

'In the sailors' dugout, your Honour!' said the helpful soldier. 'Come along, sir, I'll show you the way.'

The soldier led Kozeltsov from trench to trench until they reached a small ditch in one of the trenches. In the ditch sat a sailor smoking his pipe, and behind him was a door, with a light shining through the crack.

'Can I go in?'

'I'll just let them know.' And the sailor went in. Two voices could be heard talking inside.

'If Prussia goes on maintaining its neutrality,' one voice was saying, 'then Austria will do the same.'

'What does Austria matter,' said the other, 'when the Slav lands... All right, show him in.'

Kozeltsov had never been in this dugout. He was amazed by its ostentatious elegance. There was a parquet floor, and the door was hidden behind little screens. Two beds stood against the walls, and in one corner there hung a large icon of the Virgin Mary in a gold frame, with a pink icon lamp burning before it. A naval officer was lying asleep, fully dressed, on one of the beds; the two men who had been talking—the new regimental commander and his adjutant—were sitting on the other, at a table on which stood two opened bottles of wine. Kozeltsov was certainly no coward, and had nothing to fear either from the authorities or the regimental commander, who used to be a companion of his; and yet he felt intimidated, so haughtily did this colonel rise to his feet and wait to hear what he had to say. Kozeltsov felt his knees trembling. He was further disconcerted by the adjutant, who sat there with a look and an attitude that seemed to say 'I'm only a friend of your regimental commander. You're not reporting to me, and I have no right nor any wish to expect deference from you.' 'How odd,' thought Kozeltsov, looking at his colonel; 'only seven weeks since he took command of the regiment, and yet everything about him—his uniform, his bearing, his expression—proclaims the authority of a regimental commander: authority founded not so much on his age, or seniority in the service, or military prowess, as on his wealth. Not so long ago,' he thought, 'this same Batrischev was getting drunk with us, wearing the same cheap cotton shirt for weeks on end, and eating his everlasting meatballs and dumplings alone in his room... But look at him now! There's a white Holland shirt showing under his thick overcoat with those wide sleeves, he's smoking a ten-rouble cigar and there's a six-rouble bottle of Lafite on the table—all bought at incredible prices from the quartermaster at Simferopol—and that expression of cold pride in his eyes, as an aristocrat of wealth, which tells you: "I may be your comrade, since I'm a regimental commander of the new school, but never forget that what you've got is sixty roubles, one third of your pay, while I have tens of thousands passing through my hands—and believe me, I know full well that you'd give half your life just to be where I am!"'

'Took you quite a while to recover, didn't it?' the colonel said to Kozeltsov, casting him a cold glance.

'My wound was quite a bad one, Colonel. It's not fully healed yet, even now.'

'Then you shouldn't be here,' said the colonel, looking suspiciously at the officer's stocky figure. 'But you're fit for duty, are you?'

'Yes, sir, of course I am, sir.'

'Delighted to hear it. So you'll take over the 9th company from Ensign Zaitsev—your old company. You'll get your orders right away.'

'Yes, sir.'

'And when you go, be so good as to send the regimental adjutant over to me,' said the regimental commander, with a slight bow to indicate that the audience was over.

Coming out of the dugout, Kozeltsov mumbled something again and again under his breath, hunching his shoulders as if something was either hurting, embarrassing or annoying him. He was not annoyed with the regimental commander (there was no reason why he should be), but dissatisfied with himself and everything about him. Discipline, and what it brings with it—that is to say, subordination—is only acceptable (and this goes for any other relationship imposed by law) where it is based not only on a mutual acceptance of its necessity, but also on the subordinate's acknowledgement that his superior has greater experience, greater military prowess, or even just greater moral qualities. But as soon as discipline is founded, as so often happens in our society, on casual chance or the money principle, it always degenerates into self-importance on the one side, and concealed envy and resentment on the other. The result is that discipline, instead of usefully uniting a mass of men into a single unit, produces exactly the opposite effect. A man who finds himself unable to inspire respect by virtue of his own intrinsic merits instinctively fears close contact with his subordinates, and does his best to ward off criticism by assuming the outward trappings of importance. And his subordinates, seeing only this superficial aspect of the man and finding it offensive, are apt to conclude—usually unjustly—that nothing good lies behind it.

16

BEFORE GOING to join his fellow officers, Kozeltsov went to greet his company and see where it was stationed. The parapets built up of gabions, the arrangement of the trenches, the cannon he passed on his way, even the unexploded mortar bombs and bomb fragments he stumbled over as he walked—all these things, lit up by the unceasing flashes of gunfire, were very familiar. All this had been vividly etched into his memory three months before, when he had spent two weeks on end on this same bastion. Although that recollection had much that was very terrible, it seemed to bring with it something of the charm of the past, and he found pleasure in recognizing familiar places and objects, as though the two weeks he had spent here had been quite enjoyable. The company was deployed along the defensive wall extending to the 6th bastion.

Kozeltsov entered the long dugout, completely unprotected on the near side, in which he had been told the 9th company was stationed. The whole dugout was so full of soldiers, from the entrance in, that there was literally nowhere to put one's foot on the ground. At one end of it there was a crooked tallow candle burning, held by a soldier lying on the ground. Another soldier was reading a book, slowly spelling out the words by the light of the candle and holding the book right up to it. In the stinking half-darkness of the dugout, raised heads could be seen avidly listening to the reader. The book was a primer, and as he entered the dugout, he heard these words:

'Fear... of death is an... inborn sense... in man.'

'Trim the wick!' said a voice. 'That's a great book.'

'My... Lord...' the reader went on.

When Kozeltsov asked if the sergeant-major was there, the reader stopped and the soldiers began to stir, coughing or blowing their noses as an audience always does when it has spent a long time keeping silent. The sergeant-major stood up near the group of men surrounding the reader, buttoned his uniform, and treading across some men's legs and onto the legs of others who had nowhere to move them, came over to his officer.

'Greetings, Sergeant! So is this the whole of our company?'

'Greetings, your Honour! And welcome back!' answered the sergeant-major, looking at Kozeltsov in a cheerful, friendly way. 'How has your recovery gone, your Honour? Well, and God be thanked! We've been missing you badly.'

It was immediately obvious that Kozeltsov was popular with his company. Voices could be heard in the depths of the dugout, saying: 'Our old company commander's back, him that was wounded—Kozeltsov, Mikhail Semyonich,' and the like. Some of the men even came over to him, and the drummer greeted him.

'Hello, Obanchuk!' said Kozeltsov. 'Still in one piece?' And then, raising his voice, 'Good day, lads!'

'Good health, sir!' came a roar in response.

'How are you doing, lads?'

'Badly, your Honour. The French are beating us, giving us a proper pasting from behind their defences—but that's it—they won't come out and fight.'

'You never know—God willing, they may come out after all now I'm here,' said Kozeltsov. 'You and I, we've thrashed them before, and we'll thrash them again.'

'We'll do our best, your Honour,' several voices spoke up.

'He's really plucky, our captain is—proper brave, he is!' said the drummer, not loudly but enough to make himself heard by another soldier; as though backing up his company commander's words and reassuring his fellow soldier that there was nothing boastful or far-fetched in what he said.

Leaving his soldiers in their dugout, Kozeltsov went over to the fortified barracks to join his fellow officers.

17

THE BIG ROOM in the barracks was filled with men—naval, artillery and infantry officers. Some were sleeping; others had sat down on a packing case or a gun carriage to talk together; yet others—the biggest and noisiest group—had spread out two cloaks on the ground behind the arch and were sitting on them, drinking porter and playing cards.

'Aha! Kozeltsov, Kozeltsov! Great to see you back, good for you!.. How's the wound?' came voices from every side. And here, too, it was apparent that he was well liked and everyone was glad to see him back.

After shaking hands with the men he knew, Kozeltsov joined one noisy group of officers who were playing cards; some of them, too, were his friends. A lean, handsome man with brown hair, a long, thin nose and a thick moustache extending into his side whiskers, was dealing the cards with his long thin fingers, one of which bore a heavy gold seal ring. He was dealing fast and carelessly, obviously tense about something and trying to hide the fact by appearing unconcerned. Beside him on his right, propped up on his elbows, lay a grey-haired major who had already had plenty to drink; with affected indifference, he was playing for fifty-kopek stakes and paying on the nail. To the dealer's left was a small, perspiring, red-faced officer, squatting on his haunches, who put on a forced smile and joked every time he lost; he was constantly fumbling with one hand in the empty pocket of his baggy trousers, and playing for high stakes, but not in ready money; this was obviously what was annoying the handsome brown-haired dealer. A thin, pale-complexioned, bald and clean-shaven officer with a cavernous, cruel mouth kept pacing about the room holding a big wad of banknotes; every now and then he would stake the whole wad against the bank, and win.

Kozeltsov drained a glass of vodka and sat down with the players.

'Come on, take a hand, Mikhail Semyonich!' said the dealer. 'I bet you've brought loads of money with you.'

'Where would I get money? Not at all, I spent the last of it in town.'

'Go on! You can't have failed to fleece someone at Simferopol.'

'No, really, I haven't much,' said Kozeltsov. But he evidently did not mean the others to believe him, so he unbuttoned his coat and picked up the old cards.

'Why not give it a try, see what tricks the devil can play… sometimes even a gnat can try something on. I just need a drink to get my courage up.'

And very shortly, after another three vodkas and several glasses of porter, he felt completely in tune with the rest of the company—that is, in a state of mental fog and oblivion of reality—and was busy losing his last three roubles.

Meanwhile the perspiring little officer had a debt of a hundred and fifty roubles chalked up against him.

'No, I'm out of luck,' he said, carelessly preparing a fresh card.

'Be so good as to pay up what you owe,' said the dealer, interrupting the deal for a moment and glancing at him.

'Allow me to pay up tomorrow,' said the perspiring officer, standing up and rummaging vigorously through his empty pocket.

'Hmm!' growled the dealer, viciously flicking the cards to his right and left till the end of the pack. 'But we can't go on like this,' he went on when he had finished dealing. 'That's my lot. We can't go on like this, Zakhar Ivanich—we've been playing cash down, not on tick.'

'Why, are you doubting my word? That's very odd, I must say!'

'Where am I supposed to get my winnings?' muttered the major, by now thoroughly drunk; he had won about eight roubles. 'I've paid up over twenty roubles, but when I win, I don't get anything.'

'How can I pay you when there's no money on the table?' demanded the dealer.

'That's not my concern!' shouted the major, getting to his feet. 'I'm playing with you, honest men—not with that one.'

The perspiring officer suddenly lost his temper. 'I told you I'd pay up tomorrow! How dare you use that insulting language to me?'

'I'll say what I like! That's no way for an honest man to behave, that's what!' shouted the major.

'That'll do, Fyodor Fyodorich!' they all started saying at once, trying to restrain the major. 'Let it be!'

But it looked as if the major was only waiting to be implored to calm down so as to whip himself into a towering rage. Jumping up, he staggered over towards the perspiring officer.

'Insulting language, eh? I'm older than you, I've served my Tsar for twenty years… Insulting, am I? You scruffy little schoolboy!' he suddenly screeched, growing more and more worked up by the sound of his own voice. 'You bounder!'

But let us quickly draw a veil over this profoundly distressing scene. Tomorrow, perhaps, or even today, each one of these men will go out proudly and cheerfully to face his death, and will die with firmness and composure; but the one consolation of life, under these conditions which terrify even the coolest mind—conditions in which everything human has vanished and no escape is possible—the one consolation is oblivion, the abolition of awareness.

In the depths of every man's soul there burns a spark of nobility which will make a hero of him; that spark tires of glowing brightly all the time, but when the fateful moment comes, it will blaze up again and shine out upon great deeds.

18

NEXT DAY the bombardment continued with the same intensity. At around 11 in the morning, Volodya Kozeltsov was sitting with a group of battery officers, and having got to know them slightly, was taking a good look at the new faces, watching, questioning and telling his own story. He respected and quite enjoyed the artillery officers' restrained and intellectually rather pretentious conversation; while his own shy, fresh-faced, attractive appearance appealed to the officers too. The senior officer of the battery, a rather short, sandy-haired captain with a topknot and smooth temples, who had been trained according to the old artillery traditions, was a ladies' man and said to be a scholar. He questioned Volodya on his knowledge of artillery and the new inventions, gently teased him about his youth and his pretty face, and generally treated him as a father treats his son, which Volodya found very congenial. Second Lieutenant Dyadenko was a young, tousle-haired officer who went around in a tattered greatcoat and spoke with a Ukrainian accent, pronouncing all his 'o's in an un-Russian way. Although he had a very loud voice, seized every opportunity to get into acrimonious arguments with his fellow officers, and had abrupt, jerky movements, Volodya still liked him; under his rough exterior Volodya could not fail to discern that he was a very good and extremely kind human being. Dyadenko was constantly offering to help Volodya, and always trying to prove to him that the guns in Sevastopol were not correctly positioned. The only one to whom Volodya did not take a liking, though he was more polite than any of the others, was Lieutenant Chernovitsky, a man with permanently raised eyebrows who wore a frock coat which, while not new, was reasonably clean and neatly patched, and sported a gold chain across his satin waistcoat. He kept questioning Volodya about what the Tsar and the war minister were up to, describing with affected delight the feats of bravery being performed in Sevastopol, and lamenting how little patriotism one came across or what wrongheaded decrees the administration was issuing. All his talk was full of knowledge, common sense and noble feelings, but for some reason it struck Volodya as forced and unnatural. And the main thing was that, as he could see, the other officers almost never spoke to Chernovitsky. Then there was Cadet Vlang, the man Volodya had woken from sleep the day before. He hardly spoke at all, but sat modestly in a corner, laughing whenever anything amusing was said, remembering when something had been forgotten, serving the officers with vodka and rolling their cigarettes for them. It might have been Volodya's unassuming, polite manners, treating him like any other officer instead of lording it over him as a mere schoolboy, that won Vlang over; or it might have been his pleasant appearance; at all events Vlang (whom the soldiers called 'Vlanga' as though he was a female) could scarcely take his big, gentle, stupid eyes off the new officer's face. He was always anticipating and forestalling Volodya's wishes, and spent the whole time in a sort of fond ecstasy which the other officers naturally noticed and made fun of.

Before dinner the staff captain on the bastion was relieved of his duty and came to join the officers. Staff Captain Kraut was a handsome, dashing officer with fair hair and a big sandy moustache and side whiskers. He spoke excellent Russian, but too correctly and elegantly for a Russian. His military service and his life in general echoed his manner of speech: he was an excellent officer and comrade, impeccably correct where money was concerned; but simply as a man, simply because all this was too right—there seemed to be something lacking in him. Like all Russian Germans, by some strange contrast to the ideal 'German' Germans, he was an extremely practical man.

'Here he comes, our hero is back!' said the captain as Kraut blithely entered the room, swinging his arms and jingling his spurs. 'What'll you have, Friedrich Krestyanich, tea or vodka?'

'I've already ordered a glass of tea,' he replied, 'but meanwhile I might have a drop of vodka to cheer the spirits. Very good to meet you,' he said to Volodya who had stood up and bowed, 'I look forward to knowing you better. Staff Captain Kraut. The gun sergeant on the bastion told me you'd got here yesterday.'

'I'm very grateful to you for your bed—I spent the night on it.'

'But were you comfortable? It's got one leg broken, but now, with the siege on, there's no one to mend it. You have to prop it up.'

'How was your spell of duty—did it go all right?' asked Dyadenko.

'Not too bad, only Skvortsov bought it—and they "mended" one of our gun carriages for us. Smashed the side plate to bits.'

He got up and walked around. It was clear that he was overflowing with the sense of relief a man feels when he has just got out of danger.

'Well now, Dmitry Gavrilich,' he said, slapping the captain on the knee, 'how are you getting on, old boy? What about your promotion? No word yet?'

'No, nothing yet.'

'And there won't be anything, either,' said Dyadenko. 'I've already told you why.'

'So why, then?'

'Because your report wasn't worded correctly.'

'Oh, you contrary fellow!' said Kraut with a merry smile, 'a proper stubborn Ukrainian. And just to spite you, you'll end up a lieutenant.'

'No, I won't.'

'Vlang, bring me my pipe and fill it, would you?' he said to the cadet, who promptly ran off to get the pipe.

Kraut cheered them all up, told them about the bombardment, asked what had been happening while he was away, and had something to say to everybody.

19

'SO HOW'S IT GOING?' Kraut asked Volodya. 'Settled down here yet? I'm sorry, what's your name and patronymic? You know, that's how we in the artillery generally talk to one another. Got yourself a saddle horse yet?'

'No,' said Volodya, 'I'm not sure what to do. I told the captain—I don't have a horse, but I've no money either, until I get my forage and travel allowances. I'm thinking of asking the battery commander for a horse to tide me over, but I'm afraid he may refuse.'

'Who, Apollon Sergeich?' He made a sound with his lips to indicate the strongest doubt, and glanced at the captain. 'I shouldn't think so.'

'Well, and if he does refuse, there's no harm done,' said the captain. 'To tell you the truth, you don't really need a horse here. Still, we could always try. I'll ask him later.'

'What? You don't know him,' interrupted Dyadenko; 'if it was anything else, he might turn you down, but that he'd never refuse... Want to bet on it?'

'Oh, we know you, always arguing!'

'I'm arguing because I know him—he's stingy about anything else, but he'll let you have a horse because there's nothing in it for him to make him refuse.'

'What do you mean, nothing in it for him, when oats are costing him eight roubles a measure! It's worth his while not to have an extra horse to feed!'

'You should ask for Starling, Vladimir Semyonich,' said Vlang, returning with Kraut's pipe. 'That's a fine horse!'

'The one that tipped you into a ditch at Soroki, eh, Vlanga?' the staff captain laughed.

'No, why are you going on about eight roubles for oats?' Dyadenko pursued his argument, 'when he's got an allowance of ten-fifty? Obviously it's not worth his while.'

'So what, even if he had nothing left at all! I daresay when you get to be battery commander, you won't let anyone ride a horse down to town, will you!'

'When I get to be battery commander, my friend, my horses will get four measures of oats to eat. I shan't be making anything on the side, have no fear.'

'You'll live and learn,' said the staff captain. 'You'll be taking your cut, and this one,' he added, pointing to Volodya, 'when he's in command of a battery, he'll be slipping the loose change into his pocket too.'

'Why do you think he'd want to take a cut, Friedrich Krestyanich?' interrupted Chernovitsky. 'He's probably got a private income, so why should he try to profit by it?'

'No, sir, I... excuse me, Captain,' said Volodya, blushing to his ears, 'but I find that remark dishonourable.'

'Hey, hey, isn't he pugnacious!' said Kraut. 'When you make it to captain, you'll sing a different tune!'

'Never mind about that—I just think that if the money isn't mine, then I can't keep it.'

'Now listen to me, young man,' the staff captain began, in a more serious tone. 'Are you aware that when you're in command of a battery, if you manage things properly, you'll be sure to end up with a surplus of five hundred roubles in peacetime; in wartime it'll be seven or eight thousand, just on the horses alone. All well and good. The battery commander doesn't get involved in the soldiers' provisions—that's been the tradition in the artillery from time immemorial. If you're a bad manager, you won't have anything to spare. But then you've got expenses that aren't in the regulations: shoeing, that's one (he crooked one finger); medical supplies, two (he crooked another); stationery, three; spare horses are five hundred each, my friend, and remounts fifty—and you'll have to pay that, so that's four. And you have to replace the soldiers' collars, which isn't in the regulations either; and you'll spend a lot on coal, and you have to look after the officers' mess. And if you're the battery commander, you have to live decently yourself—you need a carriage, and a fur greatcoat, and all sorts of other things—this, that and the other… I could go on…'

'But the main thing,' put in the captain, who had been silent all this while, 'here's what, Vladimir Semyonich: just think of a man like myself, for instance, who's served twenty years on two hundred roubles a month, constantly short of money—shouldn't he be allowed to earn himself a crust of bread as a reward for his service to keep him in his old age—when the commission agents are making tens of thousands a week?'

'Anyway, what's the use of going on about it?' the staff captain added. 'Don't rush to judgement. Wait till you've seen a bit more service.'

Volodya, feeling dreadfully guilty and ashamed of his ill-considered comments, just mumbled something and carried on listening in silence, while Dyadenko hurled himself into the fray, full of excitement, and set about proving everyone wrong.

The argument was interrupted by the arrival of the colonel's orderly, to announce that dinner was served.

'Now just you tell Apollon Sergeich to serve us some wine today,' Chernovitsky said to the captain, buttoning up his tunic.

'Why's he so stingy with it? When we're killed, no one will have any!'

'Tell him yourself,' said the captain.

'No, you're the senior officer. It's got to be done by the book.'

20

THEY WERE IN the same room where Volodya had reported to the colonel the day before. The table had been moved out from the wall and covered with a grubby tablecloth. This time the battery commander shook hands with Volodya and asked him about Petersburg and his journey to Sevastopol.

'Well, gentlemen, those of you who are drinking vodka, help yourselves! Ensigns don't drink,' he added to Volodya with a smile.

The battery commander seemed altogether not so stern as he had been the day before; he now gave the impression of a good-natured, hospitable host and senior comrade. But despite that, all the officers, from the senior captain to the argumentative Dyadenko, showed, through the polite way in which they spoke to their commander, looking him respectfully in the eye, and the timid way they waited in line to receive their glass of vodka, that they held him in the greatest respect.

The dinner consisted of a large bowl of cabbage soup with greasy bits of beef floating in it, with huge quantities of pepper and bay leaves; and Polish *zrazy** with mustard, and spicy meat-and-potato patties with butter that was not quite fresh. There were no table napkins, the spoons were either tin or wooden ones, there were just two glasses each, and the only drink on the table

---

* A meat roulade dish.

was a decanter of water with its neck broken off. But the meal was not boring—the conversation never flagged. At first it was about the battle of Inkerman, in which the battery had taken part; everyone present described his experiences and his ideas about the reasons for their failure, falling silent when the battery commander himself began to speak. Then the talk turned naturally to the inadequate calibre of their light field guns, and to the new lightweight cannon, and here Volodya had a chance to show off his knowledge of artillery. But the conversation never touched on the present dreadful situation of Sevastopol, as if each officer had been thinking too much about this to want to say anything more. Nor was there any mention, to Volodya's surprise and dismay, of the duties he was to be assigned—as if he had arrived in Sevastopol merely in order to talk about lightweight cannon and dine with the battery commander. While they were eating, a mortar bomb fell not far from their building, shaking the floor and walls of their room like an earthquake and misting up the windows with gunpowder smoke.

'I don't suppose you see this sort of thing in Petersburg. Out here we often have surprises like that,' said the battery commander. 'Vlang, have a look and see where that one went off.'

Vlang went to see and reported that it had exploded in the square. Nothing more was said about the bomb.

Just before the end of the meal, the old man who was the battery clerk came into the room with three sealed envelopes, which he handed to the battery commander. 'This one here is very urgent, sir, a Cossack just brought it over from the commander of artillery,' he said. The officers could not help staring with impatient curiosity at the battery commander's practised fingers as they broke the seal and drew the *very urgent* paper out of the envelope. 'What could it be?' they all wondered. It might be orders for a complete withdrawal from Sevastopol to the rear, or for the whole battery to go to the bastions.

'Not again!' said the battery commander, angrily flinging the paper to the floor.

'What does it say, Apollon Sergeich?' asked the senior officer.

'They want an officer and crew for some mortar battery out there. I've only got four officers, and there isn't one complete crew in the whole line,' growled the battery commander, 'but here they are, demanding more. Still, gentlemen,' he added after a brief silence, 'someone will have to go. They're to be at the barrier at seven... Get the sergeant-major over here. Who's to go, gentlemen? Make up your minds,' he repeated.

'This lad hasn't been anywhere yet,' said Chernovitsky, indicating Volodya.

The battery commander said nothing.

'Yes, I'd like to go,' said Volodya, feeling a cold sweat break out on his neck and back.

'No, why him?' the captain broke in. 'Of course nobody's going to refuse, but there's no need to stick your neck out. If Apollon Sergeich is leaving it to us, then let's draw lots, like last time.'

They all agreed. Kraut cut up the slips of paper, rolled them up and tipped them into his cap. The captain began being facetious, even venturing to ask the colonel to order some wine to get their courage up, as he put it. Dyadenko sat looking sullen, Volodya was smiling at something, Chernovitsky swore that he was bound to be the one, while Kraut remained perfectly calm.

Volodya was allowed to draw first. He picked up one slip which looked longer than the rest, but immediately decided to change it, and picked up another one, shorter and fatter. Unfolding it, he read the word 'Go'.

'It's me,' he said with a sigh.

'Well, God go with you. So you'll get your baptism of fire right away,' said the battery commander, with a good-natured smile at the ensign's embarrassed face. 'Only be quick about it. To cheer you up, Vlang will go with you as your gun sergeant.'

21

VLANG WAS THRILLED to be selected, ran off at once to get ready, and as soon as he was dressed he came to help Volodya, urging him to take along his camp bed, and his fur greatcoat, and his old copies of *Fatherland Notes*, and his spirit coffee-maker, and various other unnecessary things. The captain advised Volodya to start by reading what the *Handbook** said about firing mortars, and copy out from it at once the tables of angles of elevation. Volodya set himself to this task straight away, and found to his surprise and joy that although he was still a bit oppressed by his fear of danger and his even worse fear of being a coward, those feelings were much milder than the day before. Part of the reason was the urgency of his present situation and the need to act at once, but the main reason was that fear, like every other strong emotion, cannot continue for very long at the same pitch. In other words, he had already worked his way through his fear. At about seven o'clock, just as the sun was beginning to sink behind the Nikolaevsky barracks, the sergeant-major came in to report that the men were ready and waiting.

'I've given the list of names to Vlanga. You can ask him for it, your Honour,' he said.

Some twenty artillerymen armed with broadswords but no other equipment were standing waiting round the corner of the

* *Handbook for Artillery Officers*, published by Bezak. [*Note by Tolstoy*]

house. Volodya went over to them with the cadet. 'Should I give them a little speech, or just say "Hello, lads!"—or say nothing at all?' he wondered. 'No, why shouldn't I say "Hello, lads!"—I'm sure that's what I ought to do.' And he bravely gave a ringing shout of 'Hello, lads!' The soldiers answered cheerfully; his fresh young voice made a good impression on all of them. Volodya marched boldly off at the head of his men, and although his heart was pounding as if he had just run a few miles at top speed, he marched with a light step and a cheerful face. When they approached the Malakhov mound and started up the hill, he noticed that Vlang, who never lagged behind him and who had seemed such a brave fellow back at the barracks, was constantly dodging to one side now and ducking his head, as though all the bombs and cannonballs—which were now coming thick and fast, whistling through the air nearby—were making straight for him. Some of the young soldiers were acting the same way, and most of them wore an expression if not of fear, then at least of apprehension. All this thoroughly reassured and encouraged Volodya.

'So here I am, on the Malakhov mound, and it's not such a terrible place as I expected! And I'm able to walk on without ducking away from the cannonballs—and I'm far less frightened than the others! So does that mean I'm not a coward?' he thought delightedly, even with a triumphant sense of self-satisfaction.

But his feeling of fearlessness and self-satisfaction was soon shaken by the spectacle that met his eyes in the twilight that evening on the Kornilov battery, where he had gone to try to find the bastion commander. Four sailors were standing by the parapet, holding the bloody corpse of a man, with no boots or greatcoat, by its arms and legs, swinging him through the air to fling him over the parapet. (On this second day of the bombardment, there was no time to pick up the bodies lying on the bastions; instead they were being thrown into the moat so that they did not get in the way of the gun crews.) Volodya froze for a moment, watching the corpse hitting the top of the parapet and slowly rolling down into the moat. But luckily for him, the bastion commander found him at this point, gave him his orders and assigned someone to guide him to his battery and the dugout for his gun crew. I shall not describe all the other horrors, dangers and disenchantments that our hero passed through on that evening—how, instead of the mortar fire he had observed on Volkovo Field, with all the discipline and precision he had been hoping to see here, he found two cracked little mortars with no sights, one of which had had its muzzle crushed by a cannonball, while the other was standing on the splinters of its smashed platform; how he was unable to find a working party to repair the platform until morning; how not a single mortar bomb was of the correct weight as specified in the *Handbook*; how two men in his crew were wounded, and he himself came within a hair's breadth of death some twenty times. Luckily for him, he was assigned an amazingly tall naval gunner to assist him, and this man, who had been handling the mortars from the very beginning of the siege, reassured him that these two could still be fired; he showed him over the whole bastion in the dark by the light of a lantern, as though it was his own kitchen garden, and promised to have everything working by next morning.

The dugout to which his guide took him was an oblong pit dug in the stony ground, about eight cubic yards in size, covered by two-foot-thick oak beams. This was where he took shelter with all his men. As soon as Vlang caught sight of the low entrance to the dugout, he rushed ahead and flung himself into it before anyone else, almost injuring himself on the stone floor, and cowered away in a corner from which he did not emerge. Volodya, however, waited for all the soldiers to find places for themselves on the floor next to the walls, where some of them lit their pipes; then he set up his camp bed in a corner, lit a candle, touched his cigarette to it and lay down to smoke.

Above the dugout they could hear the constant rattle of gunfire, not too loud apart from one cannon standing very close by, which shook the dugout so hard that earth showered down through the wooden ceiling. In the dugout itself all was quiet; the only sounds came from the soldiers, still too shy of their new officer to do more than exchange an occasional remark, asking one of their number to move aside, or getting a light for a pipe; or from a rat scratching about somewhere among the stones; or from Vlang, who had not yet fully recovered and was still staring wildly around, now and then heaving a loud sigh. Volodya, lying on his camp bed in his crowded corner, lit by a single candle, was experiencing the same cosy sensation he had known as a child, when, during a game of hide-and-seek, he would creep into a cupboard or under his mother's skirts, hold his breath and listen, feeling scared of the dark but at the same time enjoying it all. He was now feeling a bit uneasy, but excited too.

22

AFTER NO MORE than ten minutes the soldiers had recovered their spirits, and conversations had broken out. The most important of the men had gravitated closest to the officer's bed and candle: there were two gun sergeants, one an elderly grey-haired man with a full house of medals and crosses, save for the St George Cross, and the other a young man, a Kantonist,* who rolled and smoked his own cigarettes. The drummer, as always, had assumed the duty of serving his officer. The bombardiers and holders of the St George Cross were sitting not far away, while the humble ordinary mortals huddled together in the shadows by the entrance. It was among them that the conversation started, provoked by the noise of someone tumbling hurriedly in through the entrance of the dugout.

'What's up, mate—don't you like it out of doors? Were the girls singing something dreary?' asked one voice.

'They're playing such weird songs, I never heard the like back home,' the new arrival laughed.

'No, our Vasin's not fond of the bombs, not one bit!' said someone from the aristocrats' corner.

'Well, when there's some sense to them, that's quite another matter!' came the slow voice of Vasin. Whenever he spoke, everyone

* Kantonists were the sons of soldiers, enrolled as children in special Kantonist schools in preparation for a life of military service.

else stopped. 'On the 24th, they were firing like this because they were in trouble; but now we're being pasted for a load of shit, and the high-ups would never dream of saying "thank you" to any of us.'

'Melnikov, now—I bet he's still out there,' said someone.

'Fetch him in here, that Melnikov,' said the old gun sergeant. 'Or they really will get him, and there's no sense in that.'

'Who's Melnikov?' asked Volodya.

'Oh, one of our soldiers, your Honour, he's a bit dim-witted. He's not scared of anything at all, and now he's always wandering around outside. You ought to see him—looks just like a bear.'

'He knows a magic spell,' came Vasin's slow voice from the other corner.

Melnikov came into the dugout. He was plump (something very rare among soldiers), red-haired and red-faced, with an enormous bulging forehead and prominent pale-blue eyes.

'What's this—not afraid of the bombs, is that right?' Volodya asked him.

'Why should I be?' replied Melnikov, shifting his body and scratching his head. 'I'll never be killed by a bomb, I know that.'

'So would you like to live here, then?'

''Course I would. It's fun here!' he said, bursting into giggles.

'Oh, then they ought to take you out on a sortie! Shall I tell the general?' said Volodya, although he did not know a single general here.

''Course I'd like that! Yes!'

And Melnikov vanished among the other men.

'Come on, boys, who's for a game of "noses"? Anyone got a pack of cards?' his voice could be heard rattling out.

And soon a card game was under way in the far corner—the sounds of noses being rapped with cards, laughter and the calling of trumps could be heard. Volodya drank some tea from the samovar which the drummer had lit for him, offered some to the gun sergeants, joked and chatted with them, trying to make himself popular and very content with the respect with which they treated him. The common soldiers too, when they realized that this 'master' was a right one, joined the conversation. One of them declared that the siege of Sevastopol was soon going to end, that a friend of his in the navy who knew about things had told him that Co'stantine, the Tsar's brother, was coming to their rescue with the 'Merican fleet; and there would soon be a truce and a two-week ceasefire to let everyone have a rest, and if anyone fired, there'd be a fine of seventy-five kopeks per shot.

Vasin, who, as Volodya had had time to see, was a short man with side whiskers and big, gentle eyes, began talking about his recent leave at home, at first to general silent attention and then to laughter. At first, he said, they were glad to see him back, but then his father started sending him out to work in the fields, and the chief forester's lieutenant used to send his carriage over to pick up Vasin's wife. All this enormously amused Volodya. Not only did he not feel the slightest fear or discomfort from the overcrowding and bad smell in the dugout, he was having an extremely cheerful and enjoyable time.

Many of the soldiers were snoring by now. Vlang had also stretched out on the floor, and the old gun sergeant had spread out his greatcoat and was now crossing himself and muttering his bedtime prayers, when Volodya took it into his head to get out of the dugout and have a look at what was going on outside.

'Move your legs!' the soldiers shouted to one another as soon as he stood up; and legs were drawn in to let him pass.

Vlang, who had seemed to be sleeping, suddenly raised his head and grabbed hold of the skirts of Volodya's greatcoat.

'Stop, don't go out, how can you!' he implored him in a tearful voice. 'You don't know what it's like yet—cannonballs are landing there all the time. You're better off in here.'

But in spite of Vlang's entreaty, Volodya climbed out of the dugout and sat down at the entrance, where Melnikov was already sitting changing his boots.

The air was clean and fresh—especially after the dugout—and the night was clear and calm. Through the rolling gunfire they could hear the wheels of the carts delivering more gabions, and the voices of the men working at the powder magazine. Overhead was the distant starry sky, endlessly criss-crossed by the fiery tracks of bombs; a couple of feet to their left was a small opening into another dugout where one could make out the legs and backs of the sailors who lived there and hear their drunken voices; and ahead was the mound that housed the powder magazine, with stooping figures moving back and forth in front of it. On the very top of the mound, exposed to the bullets and bombs constantly whistling past, stood the tall shape of a man in a black coat, hands in pockets, treading down the earth which the other men were carrying up to him in sacks. Bombs often flew past, exploding very close to the magazine. The soldiers carrying the sacks of earth would duck or dodge aside, but the black figure never moved away, calmly treading down the earth without changing his posture.

'Who's that one in black?' Volodya asked Melnikov.

'No idea, sir. I'll go and see.'

'No, don't do that, there's no need.'

But Melnikov took no notice, got to his feet and went over to the man in black; he spent a long time standing beside him, just as calm and just as motionless as he was.

'He's in charge of the powder magazine, your Honour,' he said on his return. 'The magazine was holed by a bomb, so the infantrymen are bringing earth to repair it.'

Every now and then a shell seemed to be making straight for the entrance of the dugout. When that happened, Volodya would duck round the corner, then poke his head out again and look up at the sky to see if another one was coming. Although Vlang several times called out from the dugout, imploring Volodya to come in again, he spent some three hours sitting by the entrance, finding a kind of enjoyment in tempting fate and watching the bombs fly past. By the end of the evening he had worked out how many guns were firing, where they were situated, and where their shells were landing.

23

Early next morning, on the 27th, Volodya, feeling fresh and alert after ten hours' sleep, came out onto the step of the dugout. Vlang was about to follow him out too, but at the first sound of a bullet he leapt back inside, rolling head over heels and hitting his head against the entrance, to the general merriment of the soldiers, most of whom had also come out to get some fresh air. Only Vasin, the old gun sergeant and a few others avoided coming out into the trench—there was no holding back the rest, who had all poured out of the dugout to taste the fresh morning air after the stench of the dugout. Although the bombardment was just as intense as the day before, they settled down either near the entrance or by the parapet. Melnikov had been strolling around the batteries ever since daybreak, every now and then casting an indifferent glance up at the sky.

Beside the step sat two older soldiers and one young, curly-headed one, who looked like a Jew. This man picked up one of the spent bullets lying about and used a shell splinter to hammer it flat against a stone, then cut it into a cross like the St George. The other men watched him working while talking among themselves. The cross turned out really very handsome.

'You know, if we stay here much longer,' said one of the men, 'then when peace is declared, we'll all have served out our time.'

'That's right! I only had four years to go till my discharge, and by now I've spent five months in Sevastopol.'

'That doesn't count towards your discharge,' said another man. At that point a cannonball whistled overhead, landing just a few feet from Melnikov who was coming towards them along the trench.

'That one nearly killed Melnikov,' said one man.

'Won't kill me,' said Melnikov.

'Well, here's a cross for your bravery,' said the young soldier, handing Melnikov the cross he had made.

'No, my friend, a month here counts as a year's service, there was a decree said so,' the conversation went on.

'Say what you like, but when this is over there'll be the Tsar's review in Warsaw, and if we're not discharged, we'll be sent on indefinite leave.'

Just then a ricocheting bullet whined past just above their heads and struck a stone.

'You watch it, or you'll be getting your final discharge before the day's out,' said one of the soldiers.

Everyone laughed.

Without even waiting for the day's end, within the next two hours two of the men had got their 'final discharge' and five others were wounded; but the rest went on cracking jokes as before.

As promised, by morning the two mortars had been restored to usable working order. Around ten o'clock, having received an order from the bastion commander, Volodya summoned his team and led them out to the battery.

As soon as his men got down to work, they shook off every vestige of the fear they had shown the day before. Only Vlang could not pull himself together, but went on dodging and ducking as much as ever; Vasin, too, had lost some of his composure and was constantly fussing and cowering down. Volodya, however, was in a transport of enthusiasm, never giving a thought to the danger.

His delight in carrying out his duty creditably, his realization that he was no coward but actually very brave, the feeling that he was in command, and the presence of twenty men who, he knew, were eyeing him with curiosity, had made a dashing young hero of him. He even began showing off how brave he was, flaunting himself in front of the soldiers, getting up onto the banquette and unbuttoning his greatcoat to make himself more conspicuous. The bastion commander, who was just then doing the rounds of what he called his empire, had indeed got used to every kind of bravery during his eight months' service, but even he could not help admiring this handsome young lad in his unbuttoned greatcoat, revealing a red shirt and collar round his soft white neck, with his face and eyes on fire, clapping his hands and shouting 'Mortar one! Mortar two!' and then leaping gaily up onto the parapet to see where his bombs had landed. At half-past eleven the firing stopped on both sides, and at exactly twelve noon the assault on Malakhov Hill bastions 2, 3 and 5 began.

24

AROUND MIDDAY, on the Russian-held side of the bay between Inkerman and the northern fortification, two naval officers were standing on the top of the telegraph hill. One was scanning Sevastopol through a telescope; the other had just ridden up to the signal post accompanied by his Cossack orderly.

The sun was shining high and bright over the bay, which glittered warmly and cheerfully with its ships at anchor and its moving sails and boats. A light breeze barely stirred the withered leaves of the scrub oaks near the telegraph mast, raising a gentle swell in the bay below and filling the sails of the little boats. Across the bay one could see Sevastopol, looking just the same as ever, with its unfinished church, its column, its seafront, the green boulevard on the hillside and the fine library building; with its little azure inlets filled with masts, the picturesque arches of the aqueducts and the clouds of blue gunpowder smoke, lit up now and then by the crimson glow of gunfire; still the same beautiful, festive, proud Sevastopol, enclosed on one side by the yellow, misty hills, and on the other by the bright-blue sea that glittered in the sunlight. Far on the horizon, over the sea, a streak of black smoke from some steamship drifted through the air, below the long white clouds that were crawling towards the shore and promising wind. All along the line of the fortifications, especially in the hills on the left, compact clumps of dense white smoke kept suddenly appearing, several at a time, accompanied by lightning flashes that showed up even in the midday sunlight; they spread out, taking on all kinds of shapes, rising up in the air and turning dark when they reached the sky. These clumps of smoke kept appearing, now here, now there, among the hills, over the enemy batteries, in the town and high in the sky. The sounds of the explosions never stopped; the air shook with their constant reverberation…

Around noon the puffs of smoke began to appear less and less often, and the air was less shaken by the roar.

'But the second bastion's not returning fire at all any more,' said the hussar officer on horseback. 'They've been smashed to pieces! This is terrible!'

'Yes, and the Malakhov's just returning one shot for every three of theirs,' said the officer with the telescope. 'It really drives me mad, the way they're not answering fire. There's another one—landed right on the Kornilov battery, and they're not firing back.'

'But look—I was telling you, they always stop firing when it gets to around twelve o'clock. Same thing today. We'd better go and have lunch… they'll be expecting us… no point going on watching.'

'Stop—leave me alone!' answered the officer looking through the telescope, staring avidly and intently at Sevastopol.

'What is it? What's up?'

'There's movement in the trenches. Dense columns of men coming out.'

'Yes, I can see them from here,' said the naval officer. 'They're moving in columns. We ought to send a signal.'

'Look, look! They've come out of the trenches!'

And indeed, even the naked eye could now make out the dark patches moving downhill from the French batteries, across the gully, and up towards the Russian bastions. Ahead of those patches one could see dark streaks coming very close to our lines. On the bastions, puffs of white smoke shot up at a number of points, as though the firing was running all along our line. The wind brought over the sounds of a rapid exchange of gunfire, rattling like rain on a windowpane. The black streaks were moving on through the midst of the smoke, closer and closer. The noise of gunfire grew louder and louder till it merged into a continuous, rolling rumble. The puffs of smoke rose thicker and faster, spreading out along the whole line, eventually flowing together into a single lilac-coloured cloud that billowed together and drifted apart, with faint flashes and black spots just visible here and there. At last all the sounds came together in one reverberating crash.

'It's an assault!' said the officer, his face pale, passing the telescope to the naval man.

Cossacks galloped past along the road; some officers rode by, followed by the commander-in-chief in his carriage accompanied by his suite. Every face betrayed desperate anxiety and the expectation of imminent disaster.

'They can't possibly have taken it!' said the officer on horseback.

'By God, the flag! Look! Look!' said the other in a choked voice, lowering the telescope. 'French colours on the Malakhov!'

'Impossible!'

25

KOZELTSOV SENIOR, who had managed to win back all his money overnight and then lose it all again, including the gold pieces sewn into his lapel, was still sunk in heavy, unhealthy but deep slumber early that morning, in the defensive barracks of the fifth bastion, when the fateful cry went up, and was taken up by many other voices:

'Battle alarm!'

'What are you doing, Mikhail Semyonich, sleeping now! There's an assault!' came someone's voice.

'Must be one of those schoolboys,' he said, opening his eyes and still not believing what he had heard.

But suddenly he saw an officer running from one corner of the room to another, for no apparent reason, with such a pale, terrified face that he instantly realized what was going on. The thought that he might be taken for a coward, unwilling to join his company in its hour of need, struck him with terrible force, and he ran off at full tilt to join them. The artillery fire had ceased, but the rattle of musket fire was raging furiously. Bullets were flying past, not singly like carbine rounds, but in whole swarms, like flocks of birds flying overhead in autumn. The whole area his battalion had occupied the day before was clouded in smoke, and the enemy's cries and shouts could be heard through it. Soldiers, wounded or uninjured, were running back towards him in great crowds. Running forward another thirty paces, he caught sight of his company pressed up against a wall, and recognized the face of one of his men, pale as death and terrified. The other faces were no different. The fear communicated itself to Kozeltsov too, in spite of himself, and a shiver ran down his spine.

'They've taken the Schwartz redoubt,' said a young officer through chattering teeth. 'We're done for!'

'Rubbish,' said Kozeltsov angrily; and, trying to raise his own spirits by a gesture, he drew his small, blunt iron sabre and yelled:

'Onward, boys! Hurra-a-ah!'

His voice was so loud and resonant that even he himself was aroused by it. He ran ahead along the traverse, and some fifty soldiers followed him with shouts and cries. When they emerged beyond the end of the traverse and onto open ground, the bullets poured down on them like hail; two of them struck him, but where, and what they had done to him—whether they had just bruised him or wounded him—he had no time to find out. Ahead of him, through the smoke, he could now see blue coats and red trousers, and heard shouts that were not Russian. One Frenchman was standing on the parapet, waving his cap and shouting. Kozeltsov was convinced he was about to be killed, but this very thought filled him with courage. He ran further and further forward. A number of his soldiers overtook him, and others appeared from somewhere to the side, also running. The blue uniforms kept their distance, retreating from him towards their trenches; but as he ran, he kept stepping on the bodies of dead or wounded men. When he got as far as the outermost ditch, all those men became jumbled together in his eyes, he felt a pain in his chest, and sitting down on the banquette, he looked through one of the embrasures to see, to his great delight, that crowds of the men in blue coats were fleeing in confusion back to their trenches, leaving their dead lying motionless and their wounded crawling along, all in red trousers and blue coats, strewn over the whole field.

Half an hour later he was lying on a stretcher near the Nikolaev barracks; he knew that he was wounded, but felt hardly any pain. All he wanted was a cooling drink, and to be allowed to lie still in peace.

A small, fat doctor with bushy black side whiskers came over to him and unbuttoned his greatcoat. Kozeltsov looked down over his chin to see what the doctor was doing to his wound, and watching the doctor's face; but he still felt no pain. The doctor pulled Kozeltsov's shirt down to cover the wound, wiped his fingers on the skirts of his coat, and without a word or a glance at him, moved over to another patient. Kozeltsov's eyes mechanically followed what was going on around him. Remembering what had happened on the 5th bastion, he reflected with profound joy and pride that he had discharged his duty well; for the first time in all his service, he had acted as well as he possibly could have done, and had nothing to reproach himself with. The doctor, who was now applying a dressing to another officer's wound, pointed to Kozeltsov and said something to a priest with a big red beard who was standing nearby holding a cross.

'What is it? Am I going to die?' Kozeltsov asked the priest when he came over.

Without answering, the priest said a prayer and offered the cross to the wounded man.

Kozeltsov was not frightened of death. He took the cross in his feeble hands, pressed it to his lips and wept.

'So, have the French been beaten off everywhere?' he asked the priest.

'Yes, we have been victorious everywhere,' said the priest in a Ukrainian accent, pronouncing all his 'o's. To avoid distressing the wounded man, he kept from him the fact that the French colours were already flying on Malakhov Hill.

'Thank God for that, thank God,' said the wounded man, not feeling the tears flowing down his cheeks, but full of the inexpressible joy of knowing that he had acted like a hero.

For a brief instant he remembered his brother. 'God grant him the same happiness,' he thought.

26

But a different fate awaited Volodya. He was listening to a story Vasin was telling when a shout went up: 'The French are coming!' In an instant the blood drained from Volodya's head to his heart, and he felt his cheeks grow cold and pale. For a second or so he remained motionless; but looking around, he saw the soldiers buttoning up their greatcoats fairly calmly and clambering out of the dugout one by one. One of them—he thought it was Melnikov—even joked:

'Don't forget to welcome them with bread and salt, boys!'

Volodya climbed out of the dugout, closely followed by Vlang, who stuck close behind him all the way, and ran to the battery. There was no artillery fire from either side. Volodya's spirits rose, not so much at the sight of the men's calm as that of the cadet's pathetic, undisguised cowardice. 'I can't possibly be like him, can I?' he thought, running cheerfully up to the parapet where his mortars were standing. He could clearly see the French running across the open ground to the bastion, and crowds of them moving about in the nearest trenches, their bayonets glinting in the sun. One of them, a short, broad-shouldered soldier in a Zouave uniform, was racing ahead of the rest, sword in hand, leaping over the shell holes. 'Fire grapeshot!' Volodya shouted, leaping down from the banquette; but the soldiers had not waited for his order, and the metallic hiss of grapeshot hissed above his head, first from one mortar and then the other. 'First mortar! Second mortar!' he commanded, running through the smoke from one mortar to the other and completely oblivious of the danger. To one side he could hear the nearby rattle of Russian covering fire and the men's anxious shots.

Suddenly a piercing cry of despair sounded from the left, and was taken up by other voices: 'They're coming from behind! From behind!' Volodya looked round. Some twenty French soldiers had appeared behind them. One of them, a handsome black-bearded man in a red fez, was running ahead of the rest, but when he got to within ten paces of the battery, he stopped, fired, and then ran on. For a second Volodya stood still as though turned to stone, unable to believe his eyes. When he came to himself and looked about, he saw blue uniforms ahead of him on the parapet; one man had even jumped down and was spiking one of the guns. There was no one left near him but Melnikov, killed by a bullet just beside him, and Vlang, who had grabbed hold of a handspike and was rushing forward with lowered eyes and an expression of fury on his face. 'Follow me, Vladimir Semyonich! Follow me! We're done for!' came Vlang's despairing voice, as he brandished the handspike at the Frenchmen who were coming at them from the rear. The French soldiers did not know what to make of this enraged figure. He struck down the Frenchman in front of him with a blow on the head, the rest faltered and did not know what to do next, and Vlang, constantly looking over his shoulder and desperately yelling 'Follow me, Vladimir Semyonich! What are you waiting for? Run!', raced on to the trench where our infantry were sheltering and firing at the French. Jumping down into the trench, he leant out of it to see what his adored ensign was doing. Something in a greatcoat was lying face downwards on the spot where Volodya had been, and the whole area was now occupied by French soldiers, who were firing at our men.

27

Vlang found his battery on the second line of the defences. Out of the twenty who had manned the mortar battery, only eight had survived.

By nine that evening Vlang and his battery were on a steamship loaded with soldiers, cannon, horses and wounded men, on their way to the North Side. There was no firing anywhere. The stars shone brightly in the sky, as they had done the night before; but a strong wind was raising a swell on the sea. On the first and second bastions, flashes of lightning ran along the ground, explosions rent the air, illuminating strange black objects and rocks that flew up into the air. Something was on fire by the docks, and the red flames were reflected in the water. The pontoon bridge, crowded with people, was lit up by the glare from the Nikolaev battery. A mass of flames seemed to float above the water by the distant headland where the Alexander battery was situated, lighting up the underside of the cloud of smoke that hung above it. And just like the day before, the same calm, defiant lights shone over the sea from the faraway enemy fleet. The fresh breeze stirred up the surface of the bay. In the glow of the various fires, one could see the masts of our scuppered ships, sinking slowly ever deeper into the water. There was no talking on deck; over the regular beat of the waves and the hiss of steam one might hear the horses snorting and stamping in the tow barge, the captain giving his commands and the groans of the wounded men. Vlang, who had had nothing to eat all day, got a piece of bread out of his pocket and began chewing it; but when he suddenly remembered Volodya, he burst out into such loud sobs that the soldiers near him could hear.

'Look at him—eating bread and crying all at the same time, our Vlanga,' said Vasin.

'Weird!' said another. 'Look, they've set fire to our barracks too,' he went on, and sighed. 'How many of our lot died there—and then the French got it for nothing!'

'Well, at least we got out of it alive—and thank the Lord for that!'

'Even so, it's a shame!'

'What's a shame? Is he going to have himself a good time here? Not a bit of it! Just you wait, our lot will get it back. However many of us have to die, as God's my witness, if the Tsar gives the order, we'll get it back! Are we just going to let them have it? Never! Here you are, then,' he went on, addressing the French now, 'here's the bare walls for you, but we've blown up all the breastworks. All right, you've stuck your flag up on the Malakhov, but you're keeping clear of the town. You wait, we'll deal with you good and proper—just give us time,' he concluded.

'You bet we will!' said the other, full of conviction.

Right along the line of the Sevastopol bastions, which had teemed with such extraordinary life and energy for months on end, seeing its heroes dying one after another, to be replaced by others who died in their turn; and which had for so many months filled the enemy forces with fear, hatred and lately admiration—on these Sevastopol bastions there was now not a soul to be seen anywhere. All was dead, laid waste, dreadful—but not silent. The destruction was still going on. The ground was torn up by fresh explosions, loose soil scattered everywhere, with twisted gun carriages lying on top of the crushed corpses of Russian and enemy soldiers; heavy cast-iron cannon, now silenced forever and hurled with terrifying force into shell craters where they lay half buried under piles of earth; bombs, cannonballs, more corpses, craters, split wooden beams, dugouts, and more and more silent corpses in grey and blue greatcoats. And all of this still shuddered and gleamed under the crimson glow of the explosions which even now continued to shake the air.

The enemy could see that something incomprehensible was going on in the dread city of Sevastopol. Those explosions, and the deathly silence on the bastions, made them shudder; but after the strong, resolute resistance they had encountered all day, they still dared not believe that their implacable foe had disappeared. Without moving, they silently and fearfully awaited the end of that gloomy night.

The Sevastopol force surged together and ebbed apart like the sea on a dark, restless night; shifting uneasily throughout its huge mass, it swayed along the bay and over the bridge to the North Side, moving slowly through the impenetrable darkness, away from that place where it had left behind so many courageous brothers—away from that place now drenched with its blood, that place which for eleven months it had held against an enemy twice its strength, and which it had now been ordered to give up without a fight.

For every Russian, that order came at first as a bitter and incomprehensible shock. That was followed by the fear of pursuit. The men felt defenceless, as soon as they had left the places they had grown used to defending; they huddled anxiously together in the darkness by the entrance to the bridge, which was rocked by a fierce wind. To the sound of clashing bayonets, the infantry crowded together, regiment by regiment, carriages and militiamen; mounted officers bearing new orders forced their way through; civilians and officers' orderlies begged in tears to be allowed to bring their baggage, which was not being let onto the bridge;

with a rumble of wheels, the artillery forced its way through to the shore, hurrying to get away.

In the midst of all their other anxious preoccupations, everyone was imbued with the instinct for self-preservation and the desire to get away as quick as could be from this dreadful place of death. This feeling was shared even by the mortally wounded soldier lying among five hundred others like him, on the stone paving of the Pavlovsky quay, begging God to grant him death; and the militiaman summoning the last of his strength to push a passage into the packed crowd, to make way for a general to get through on horseback; and the general himself, firmly in command of the crossing and restraining his soldiers' haste; and the sailor swept up by a moving battalion and barely able to breathe for the crush of swaying bodies; and the wounded officer carried on a stretcher by four soldiers, who, unable to move forward in the crush, had laid the stretcher down on the ground by the Nikolaev battery; and the artilleryman who had manned his gun for sixteen years and who now, in obedience to an order from the high command which he simply could not understand, was being helped by his comrades to heave his gun off the steep bank into the bay; and the sailors who had just finished scuttling their ships and were now rowing smartly away in their longboats. As the soldiers reached the far side of the bridge, almost every one doffed his cap and crossed himself.

But at the back of this instinct there was another one, oppressive, nagging, and much deeper than the rest: a feeling that seemed to have something of remorse, shame and fury in it. Almost every soldier, as he gazed across from the North Side to abandoned Sevastopol, sighed with a heart full of unspeakable bitterness, and shook his fist at the enemy.

St Petersburg, 27 December 1855

AVAILABLE AND COMING SOON FROM PUSHKIN PRESS CLASSICS

The Pushkin Press Classics list brings you timeless storytelling by icons of literature. These titles represent the best of fiction and non-fiction, hand-picked from around the globe – from Russia to Japan, France to the Americas – boasting fresh selections, new translations and stylishly designed covers. Featuring some of the most widely acclaimed authors from across the ages, as well as compelling contemporary writers, these are the world's best stories – to be read and read again.

MURDER IN THE AGE OF ENLIGHTENMENT
RYŪNOSUKE AKUTAGAWA

THE BEAUTIES
ANTON CHEKHOV

LAND OF SMOKE
SARA GALLARDO

THE SPECTRE OF ALEXANDER WOLF
GAITO GAZDANOV

CLOUDS OVER PARIS
FELIX HARTLAUB

THE UNHAPPINESS OF BEING A SINGLE MAN
FRANZ KAFKA

THE BOOK OF PARADISE
ITZIK MANGER

THE ALLURE OF CHANEL
PAUL MORAND

SWANN IN LOVE
MARCEL PROUST

THE EVENINGS
GERARD REVE